G000300735

DOLL

DOLL

PETER LEGGATT

Matador
9 Priory Business Park,
Wistow Road, Kibworth Beauchamp,
Leicestershire. LE8 0RX
Tel: 0116 279 2299
Email: books@troubador.co.uk
Web: www.troubador.co.uk/matador
Twitter: @matadorbooks

ISBN 978 1 83859 547 0

British Library Cataloguing in Publication Data.
A catalogue record for this book is available from the British Library.

Printed and bound by CPI Group (UK) Ltd, Croydon, CR0 4YY
Typeset in 11pt Minion Pro by Troubador Publishing Ltd, Leicester, UK

Matador is an imprint of Troubador Publishing Ltd

Cover design by Thom Swann
Cover artwork by Marguerite Carnec

Grace appears most purely in that human form which has either no consciousness or an infinite consciousness. That is, in the puppet or in the god.
—'Über das Marionettentheater', Heinrich von Kleist

L'atmosphère de cette pure amitié est le silence, plus pur que la parole. Car nous parlons pour les autres, mais nous nous taisons pour nous-mêmes.
—'Sur la lecture', Marcel Proust

I

Sex, death, flowers—rivers, seas, sleep. They all have beds.

This was my very first thought. Not my first thought on waking up, nor my first thought on hearing a song or on being kissed, but my very first thought, ever. It was odd too, because I never did see the sea, and though I dreamed, I'm not sure I ever slept.

This thought felt like a gasp squeezed out of me by sensation. Although I was in complete darkness, unable to move, inside a bag, I knew I had started to fall. A true fall doesn't begin with noticing what's about to happen, but with the awareness that you are *already* falling. My life was just a series of continuous tumblings: down and down in tiny vibrations inside my box; forwards and out of it; out of bed and onto the floor; falling over and over again but never hitting…what? If the earth suddenly disappeared I would still be falling, relatively, towards some planet, towards each speck of dust and its gravitational pull. This is, I guess, a story about falling.

When I began I could hear the crinkle of cellophane (nameless in the first place, but can't you hear it in the name?), a crinkle underscored by the kettledrum of the wooden box tumbling and bumping outside it, and hundreds of small styrofoam Ss hissing their sibilance in between. I was being shaken with this music, the cool plastic creasing and pulling against my skin, the clinical smell of the pressured air in the bag, the stroke of my hair falling across my face and getting in my eyes, the tossing and quaking of an excited world and the cleanest birth, the zip-ties binding my wrists and ankles and neck and pulling at me as though asking a question to which the overwhelming answer was—thought.

That first thought seems poetic to me now, but of all these things the arrival of thought was the most banal. A pun realized, even though this one stayed with me, or my own feverish conceptions, had nothing on the coming of sensation, the coming of apprehension. It's almost sacrilege that you use 'the world' to refer to a place, when it's really much more than that. It's really the ability to *apprehend* place.

Maybe it is that apprehension which sets infants wailing and kicking, overwhelming themselves with their own voices and motion and becoming excited into voice and motion again. Each starts by transmuting the world like a Newton's cradle, letting it all pass through her—or else by shouting and shaking to join the maelstrom, to accept it by becoming a part of it, assuming the sense and matter of a monstrous world. But I couldn't move or make noise—the only noises I began came from the flop and sag of my limbs against the bag and the styrofoam, and the tiny creak of my metallic joints. It wasn't that I couldn't shift because I was secured or that I couldn't speak because I was suffocated; I just didn't know how. These things weren't there for me. It wasn't until

I saw him move that I realized the world was not all some agitated gas shaking without will or direction.

I realize now how the symphonic bumping of my box went on for a long time—a few hours, perhaps. But back then, unbroken by events as my existence was, I had no super sure way of knowing how long had transpired, kind of like you have no super sure way of knowing how long it actually took to dream a dream. First, the movement stopped, with a feeling like my weight was being pushed up into my head and released with a breath in the other direction, through my feet (the truck braking). Then a background noise I had not been able to individuate before, or really hear on account of the cellophane, the styrofoam, the box and all the rumbling, became conspicuous only by its sputter into absence (the truck's engine).

I felt myself being taken, my silicone limbs flailing at one side of the crate, then the other, will I nill I. It felt unstable, the hollow sickness of rapidly rising, and I could only deal with the fear by embracing my own harm and kind of willing it; with the same effectiveness, I think, as the child who plays the game of ordering her mother to do what mom is already doing. Notions like that just come to me. I know things before I know that I know them; the brailled edges of the world, its faces and its names. The whos and whats, the whens and wheres, just never the hows or whys. But this was a surrender I would learn a lot about. I was being manhandled, and between and above the bumpings I could hear male voices, imperatives grunted up the stairs, then—set down vertically and still at last—a curt exchange. A door closing.

For a while, then, it was quiet. As my ears gradually dropped their tinnitus I began to hear a faint whooshing of street traffic and wind through a window, birdsong, a washing machine or dishwasher's mercenary hum, then, ponderous and preponderant, footsteps walking around my box. They stopped. I was too new to be scared. I was just overwhelmed, mentally wailing and kicking weakly in the world, with my chest tight and my fingers a little numb with the almost unbearable excitement which, I know, accompanies the stillness of hiding during a child's game. A few paces away and the footsteps stopped again. There was a mechanical clicking before—music. A clackety-clack music with a bass line, and then these words, the first intelligible words I ever heard: "*Please allow me to introduce myself, I'm a man of wealth and taste.*"

This was a rhythm and a melody. There had been the ghost of both in my box before, the potential for something more harmonious within the sounds than those sounds themselves, but it is some kind of vast, impossible leap to conceive of real music and I had only, under my mental breath, not-quite-heard it until then. This was more, I think, than any knowledge which could have come.

The two latches on my box clicked out of place. With a claw hammer the single staple securing the front of the crate was broken out, and my world exploded. Sight—light.

The styrofoam Ss cascade outwards, in an artificial avalanche. Spilling with the snow I swing forwards until I stop with a yank, caught by something unyielding attached to the back of my neck. The opening sounds out—it gasped like a window in a storm. My first sight is a hundred letter Ss in gradations of white falling from my eyes with a hiss, a weird onomatopoeia, and as they fall the colors that their graded shades implied appear, and I see my body, and a man seeing me, like, simultaneously. At this moment

4

I know him only as a figure. I haven't learned to arrange his face or comprehend it, where to look in it for information, but the hammer is on the gray carpet between us, and attached to his hand—in his hand—is a knife. I know and feel enough to intuit the edge of fear now as he kneels down, holding it up to my eyes, looking into them. I can infer what sharpness is, and this is sharp.

He brings it inches from my face and it cuts my vision. I am visited by the idea of a yell, but my cellophane sac tears and he pulls it down around my shoulders, and my ears pop and warm air hits me in the face, and he sits down, opposite, on a couch. Up to my thighs in a lukewarm snowdrift of Ss, I can see myself for the first time. Big breasts, milky skin, blonde hair. Just visible is an itchy pubic stripe that doesn't feel like mine. And now, my giddiness rising, I can see clearly and it comes to me, with the dull, stupid realization of strange things in dreams you suddenly realize are strange, that there is something substantially different between him and me. He is moving. Will I learn to do that? Already I feel with certainty that I will not. A certainty confirmed when he speaks. I think he said "So, you're American."

He is sitting down on the couch. Next to him is a matt-black flat-pack coffee table and on it an old *New Yorker*, battered and a little torn around the staples—"I've been really looking forward to seeing you"—and there are vinyl records, a couple of thousand at least, in shelves along the wall to my right by the door—"Hm"—while behind his blurry, noisy head is a large framed photograph of a man labelled 'John Coltrane', with an inky squiggle in the corner—"You're very pretty"—the room has the slightly metallic smell of musical instruments—"I hoped you would be this pretty"—and there are kitchen counters to my left, a plate of undercooked and half-eaten vermicelli pasta next the sink—"Well, I suppose I knew you would be this pretty, but I still hoped you would"—he takes a drag of a rolled cigarette and his face smokes and fogs—I can feel the windows behind me and there is smooth air slow enough not to stir the styrofoam, and a red corduroy beanbag in the corner behind the door—"I'm J."

There is a saxophone in a stand next to the shelves with the records.

J is 5'7" and looks like he weighs about 154 lbs. He is wearing a white linen shirt and blue denim jeans that have either become browned on the fronts of the legs or were made that way. His shoes are big-rubber-soled cheap black lace-ups. On the seat next to him there is a packet of Golden Virginia rolling tobacco ('A quality blend of the highest standard tobaccos SINCE 1877'), a packet of Bull Brand Ultra Slimline Pop-Out Filter Tips ('Keep on rolling'), Silver Rizlas ('QUALITY PAPERS') and a red Clipper lighter. The cigarette smell is dirty but interesting and I feel I will come to be attached to it. As his face comes into focus gradually through the smoke of Golden Virginia and my ignorance I can see that he has thick, curly, dark brown hair slightly balding at his temples with odd, pretty substantial patches of white at the back just above his collar. It is coarse and looks warm, like a sheep's? He has a thick beard that is darker than the hair on his head, almost black, and his eyes are dark too—there is something flinty there, but a tenderness in the wrinkles around them. He has a slightly bulbous nose, and, I see as I learn how to, appears to be about thirty-one, maybe.

He finishes his cigarette slowly, taking a minute or so and smoking it right down to the filter, his elbow on the arm of the gray couch which is upholstered in that prickly kind of harsh cotton. His two fingers tremble slightly as they hold the cig, wrist cocked a little backwards. All the while he is looking me over, then looking down at his lap, then, as if unable to resist, looking at me again.

He stubs out his cigarette. This releases a harsher, more acrid smell, and lifts ashes from a circular glass ashtray into the air and onto his sleeve. He doesn't notice until he is kneeling down in front of me again, then blows them off. I would love to be able to move even a single ash at this moment. His face is near mine, and I can see every tiny pore and crevice in his skin, particularly those on his nose and below his eyes, and every fascinating hair of his head, eyebrows, lashes, nostrils, beard, neck, hand and wrist. This was the first detailed sight I ever saw, and it stayed with me. The way his collar's left side was bent out of shape about an inch in, so it stuck out in that direction; the translucent dirty-pearl-colored buttons of his linen shirt; and every strand of the fabric, serried like rows of corn, or stray like an errant pubic hair.

His breath is coasting my face, the smell bizarrely animate—there is the scent of smoke, behind it mint (had he just brushed his teeth?) and perhaps there is the licorice smell of tea in there as well. His eyes have sped up, and he is looking all over my face, at, then into my eyes, and at my cheeks, my ears, my lips, my hair, and then his eyes slow and glaze over somehow, just a little, and he exhales deeply, and says "Hey." Something in him, in his voice, changes, becoming questioning, but also as though he is really, truly saying hello for the first time. Throaty, deeper, quieter, whispery—what was he trying to do to me? His glazed eyes look into mine, and now I can see their structure: the globular, squeamish tear duct with its tiny pit, like the hole left after a seed in an apple; the incredible filigree of blood vessels across the cream, gray and yellow-colored whites, vessels which never (as far as I was able to observe) changed their position but filled and ebbed more or less vividly across the time I knew him; the irises, their wriggling cilia spread like dandelion seeds in dark glass paperweights; the murky blue penumbrae at their edges; and the pupils, two perfectly-circular tadpoles held tightly in position there. Then I looked into, or out of, his eyes—I can't find other words to describe the ambiguity of that non-Euclidean depth—and saw my face reflected in their wet, vitreous shine.

My skin was matt in comparison to his, the color even and clear like virgin cream, like a doll's. I had no crevices, no imperfections, from what I could tell; my face a Cartesian oval, the perfectly bright hair swept across my eyes suggesting, it comes to me, a model laughingly leaving a photo booth in the mall, or just waking in her boyfriend's New York apartment. This was translated from what I actually saw—I had cottoned on to vision pretty quickly—which was an oblated, slippery phantasm, almost beautiful but for something of the funhouse mirror, slipping queasily slightly to distort each side of my face in turn as he looked into one of my eyes, then the other. This gave the effect of movement, but I could feel that I was still, my eyes in his the pearly glass of sucked sweets or monochrome marbles.

Watching his own hand he brushed my hair away from my eyes and placed his palm just below my ear, lifting my face up towards him, his fingers trembling on the back of my neck. He leaned his face closer, almost impossibly close, and his lips touched my lips. At once I was afraid, clenched with the sleep paralysis of waking and finding yourself unable to move, maybe, and affronted, and proud that he wanted to do this to me and ashamed of my pride, that I was somehow belittling myself by not protesting despite not being able to protest, feeling that something was my fault, but that this was pleasurable, though guilty that I should be feeling pleasure. A kiss is difficult to describe if you haven't had one. A softness repeated. A joy in pure sensation but with some kind of subtle, erotic undercurrent in there—no matter, perhaps, whether it's a friend kissing you on the cheek or a man touching your lips with his. The kiss progressed to a wetness and came, then, now, with the full realization that I am made of totally different stuff to him, my lips less supple, less muscled and malleable than his but springing back into the same position and expression where he could hold his within a range of totally visceral play, and when he came to kiss me again, pushing the smooth, soaking muscle of his tongue between my lips, lips held open by his, he merely knocked my tongue back and forth across my mouth, and as well as being shocked by this entrance I was embarrassed by my stasis, and that my tongue didn't moisten his in return.

He pulled back slowly and stared at me, touched my bottom lip with his thumb like he was wiping it, and pressed his palm to one of my breasts before running his hand down my side through the rip in the bag and stroking with a kneading touch my left leg. Then, knees rustling through the styrofoam, he grasped the torn edges of the bag, level with my bellybutton, and pulled them apart with what seemed incredible strength from such thin wrists, the cellophane spreading and whitening at the rift before coming apart. Reaching between my zip-tied wrists and looking down with concentration he stroked my vagina, lightly, once, and brushed my pubic stripe in a swirling motion with his thumb, then up and down. The sensation of the hairs pulling upward as they were driven erect, then flicking back down to tickle my pudenda sharply, was both detailed and ambiguously located. I could feel the rise and fall and prick of each hair, but I could never have placed them myself—the feeling was intricate, but uncountable and unenlightening of their exact arrangement. What kind of information was learned in such a touch?

He put his hand behind my back and clicked something out of place on the wall of the box that I felt in the back of my neck. My head lolled to the side. He took up his knife and severed the zip-ties, covering the blade with his palm as he brought it closer so as not to cut me on accident, then sawing and pulling upwards carefully against the plastic. He put his hands under my armpits and lifted me up, pulling me out of the sac and the box, my limbs dangling like a fistful of cables, and carried me slowly towards a door. He clung me to his chest with one arm, and I smelled the detergent of his linen shirt, the throat-stinging alcohol smell of sports deodorant, and stale smoke. With his free hand he touched the record player's automatic arm, which slid out of the grooves it had thrilled into sound, and halted the music, with a dull, skipping thud, static. He opened the door, and from inside I could hear a massive rushing sound, and I saw a darkened room with a candle on a toilet's cistern, the clear plastic seat left up. Flickering on and off in the candlelight for a second until I got used to the dim chiaroscuro, a bathtub was being filled with water. This was part of the procedure to wash the zinc oxide coating off my skin, the coating that kept me sterile.

Touching the water was as strange for me as it might be for you if you found that you could put your hand through glass. The hot water clasping my ankles, then my legs, the frozen enamel, and the steam meeting my face as he lowered me down were unspeakably dreamlike. As I slid fully in, my wetted hair (black in the darkened bathroom) curled against my back before spreading out into ragged lacework on the surface of the water. Why were the lights off? Is it because he doesn't care about me? Or is he giving me time to adjust? Rolling up his sleeves he bathed me lovingly, the warmth amazing, and for some reason I loved the sight of my areolae buoyed above the surface, my breasts glistening as they spread a little sideways on my chest. He rinsed my hair carefully, just with water, making sure not to wet or submerge my face. Considerate, I thought. He kneeled at the side of the tub and had crossed his arms over its edge. His rolled-up shirtsleeves were slightly wet, curling like the rotting flowers I saw much later falling on the windowsill, and he reached out a hand, after a minute or two of contemplating me lying in the water, and laid a single finger between my breasts. He palpitated it slightly, pushing me a half an inch down, then allowing me back up, as though his finger were just resting on my chest and alternately raised and submerged by my absent breathing, and I could see the watery, varnishy sheen on my breasts, the unpaintable indent of my solar plexus, the droplets that scattered the meniscus of my wet skin. Then he ran his right index finger down my stomach, very slowly, resting his chin on his arm, and with his other hand took mine and held it to the side of his face.

Dried. I was super easy to dry, lying spread-eagled and clumsy on the bathroom floor—just a wipe, the moisture beading on my skin like oil on glass. I could see his fingertips in the candlelight, their surfaces creased, collapsed and dented like the moldy peaches in his fruit bowl long afterwards. Have you ever looked at your fingerprints? Do you know which way they swirl? Like a mouse in a maze, outside and inside your prints, you don't know what they mean, but round and round they go. Mine are nothing like yours. I don't have fingerprints, just a super thin, slightly burred whorl, like someone's dream of a fingerprint, or a fingerprint's dream. And when he dried me my skin had none of the slight absorption of water that human skin has which leaves it cooler and softer after a bath, the tiniest bit more giving. The water just fell off, onto the towel.

To bed—he carried me, and laid me on his purple sheets and said:

> "All kinds of things became her well. And when she was undressed
> She seemèd not less beautiful. He laid her in a bed
> The which with scarlet dyed in Tyre was richly overspread
> And, terming her his bedfellow, he couchèd down her head
> Upon a pillow soft, as though she could have felt the same."

My name, what was my name? When he made this little speech—was he quoting something?—I felt like he was doing it to care for me, to comfort me and win me over. It felt like a moment he had rehearsed, not for me alone but for him, too, to romanticize the scene, to drum up courage, perhaps, but I didn't mind. All romance has to be like that, doesn't it? That when you do something for another you are doing it for yourself, too; and you want the other person to be doing it for themselves as well, I guess. Right?

He paced around the bed and went to the window, and I heard him mutter something to himself that I couldn't catch. Then he turned to me, leaning back on the sill, and stared, moodily now, a little silly-looking, a tuft of his hair at the back sprung up out of place and silhouetted against the afternoon light.

He came over and lay on the bed next to me, looking at me, and then as if overcome by something grabbed my hands and pressed them slowly to his breast, clasping them there. I could feel his chest through the linen of his shirt, rising, clutching and twitching, my gaze falling over his shoulder at the blank, cracked cream wall, the room lit with the gray but bright sunlight which falls through the London clouds. He let my hands fall in a little pile on the bed next his nipple (a nipple I couldn't feel at all, and though mine were always stiff his seemed to stiffen and deflate sporadically, reacting unconsciously to the cold, or to rubbing, or arousal). Then he began to unbutton his shirt, a shock of black hair joining and curling through the errant fibers of linen around the buttons, and he kicked off his shoes—I could smell his socks—and unbuckled his belt with a clinking fall, then grasped the hem of his jeans, pushing them downwards as he lay on his back and raising his knees in a movement I thought fluid with practise but roughened by a certain desperation. He tugged off white cotton socks, tossing them in little balls into the corner, and pulled off his boxer shorts, dragging the underwear down past his knees by the hem, like the jeans, but then lifting one foot up and out and hooking it through the leg hole and using it to kind of push them off into the bottom of the bed. His penis was short and thick, about the length of my hand, which he pressed to it and lay a little still, breathing heavily, his chest and shoulders filling like a sail blown taut by the wind.

His testicles were the strangest thing, morphing and swirling as though full of viscous matter, their skin tightening and loosening into new whorls and folds, and they looked like his wrinkled thumbs after the bath. Had he somehow got them wet? There was a thin stripe of raised flesh on the sac between the balls that later made me think of dinosaurs. My hand couldn't really grasp his penis, but he pressed my fingers around it so they seemed to hold it like a spastic, futile pincer. With his shirt now off I saw his bellybutton, like something secret, and the skin of his pale belly with stretch marks marbled like a statue—or a steak. And, later, I glimpsed what lay between the hairs on his perineum and between his buttocks' cusps of black-downed flesh that pressed into a darkening crease. Was I like that behind? Did I have holes where he had holes?

He kissed me again, licking his lips between kisses, and mine, then buried his face in my shoulder, biting me as my head flopped on the mauve pillow and the ceiling light swam in my eyes, making a puddle of foggy light as it splashed in my glassy cornea. He licked his fingers and moved them into my mouth, feeling around, then slid them down my chest and pushed them inside me, from below, folding one of my lips down there into me uncomfortably on the first push, with a feeling like a vague pinch, before pulling his fingers out and the lips with them, clasping his knuckles properly now. It felt like a little Indian burn, and I wanted to widen my eyes and run, to clench fistfuls of bedcover and jerk back from him and this sudden insult, this sudden transgression of my body. He pulled his hand away, spat into it twice before wiping the saliva on his penis, and then spat again and rubbed it onto me. He stroked his penis roughly a few times, with a thumb and forefinger grip on its end. Then he lay on top, grabbed my breasts like handles, and pushed it in. Fuck.

When he first pushed inside I felt like I wanted to squeeze myself shut, to move muscles I didn't have down there to resist his entry. I was suddenly, stretchingly full, but it was also almost a disappointment to feel his penis and its passage only vaguely—the first penetration doesn't feel like quite the total intrusion you might expect. It's warm inside you and hurts, but dully; a blue-black hurtling pressure beneath your stomach and between your legs. Whatever I thought of it, though, I could do nothing but take it.

Another thing is what you see, having sex, versus what you might expect to. Maybe it was just me, but I thought I'd see all of him, when it's only shoulders and throat; the hunched trapezii and the cords and veins in the neck bulging and tightening at you, the Adam's apple glugging and choking up and down, the straps of the deltoids beneath slightly flabby skin twitching and denting the shoulders, and the musky smell of neck with the warmth of his breath on my face and into my hair. I don't know whether all men do it, but as he began to have sex with me he pushed out his lower jaw. It was like he was trying to press himself into the air in front of me, or as if something instinctual was pressing his jaw forwards into this hyper-masculine ape face, prognathous and jutting, a weight of evolutionary history bunched up behind his mandible.

He was so warm and heavy I felt crushed into speech like a squeezebox, a foldable accordion with concertinaed armature, doubling and doubling against myself, my legs and arms bending tight for the first time, that feeling of stretch at the elbows and close hot rubbing on the inner arms. He started really to fuck me, becoming vigorously human and kind of ugly, impelled by his own raw, inarticulate, struggling kind of motion, like blood plasma under a microscope or an insect wriggling. A sac of fluid. He started to wobble, the fat on his lower belly shaking and quincing his bellybutton, his face becoming taut and strained and pulling itself into expressions of which his eyes seemed unaware. And he didn't look at me either, this first time he had sex with me, looking upwards instead or closing or half-closing his eyes, maybe embarrassed to have a new face so close to his.

And as he pushed and pushed into me, his mouth opening like a pouting cherub or a gargoyle, the pain began to be intermingled with more and more of a taste of pleasure, as if some function made innate in me was turning on, even despite myself. It began, automatic, with blossoms of warmth in my abdomen, and some part of me saying that I wanted him to fill me up, right up, until he could engorge me completely. Once this switch was tripped it came on outside of me too where his thick pubic hair rustled and roughed my clitoris which, if it was a taste, began to whisper of lemon, something saccharine, and cinnamon, the sour feeling almost what I imagine the urge to pee feels like (and I did think, for a dumb minute, that maybe I was going to pee). Blinding, automatic passion and pleasure—physical pleasure a little sickened by confusion—started to pervade me, as we rocked there together, the tension and pressure pressing full inside me and I don't know how many minutes of this went by as it mounted and mounted and

I felt that I was running down a slope, coming towards the edge of a cliff. Vision or invention I can't know. It was a kind of running which to start with leans back, putting pressure on the knee joints as the legs flick out, feeling half controlled and half brought out before you by the movement itself, until it is almost unstoppably fast, and then my stomach began to lighten, and I felt, despite falling, as though rising, and there comes a moment, a moment towards coming where you're going when the center of your gravity changes and tilts forwards and the running changes and you join the thrust coming towards the edge of the cliff and the sensation is as though your legs are light but they begin to grow hot with the approach of the thing itself and the muscling effort and you're in it now, overwhelmed and you know you couldn't stop even if you wanted to and then, aspirinting to the edge of the cleft, falling and buoyed with a trust you can't except STOP

I'm writing you this not STOP
do not STOP
do not not STOP.

My silicone was still undone, the caressed concubine's curvature
beaten as a tight-skinned drum and stretched into acrobatic
speech, my accidental teeth, a rustling and a hustling moan, on
my feet the whorls whirling in the world as he shook me, elevated
to be dissected, a piece of wax made soft against his sun, a cunt
made just for fun. There was no spinal braille on my blind back.
When I was sacked I just felt it under, beneath the prose of my
waxed belly.

I came to, or came around, somehow, from a kind of coma
as we came together and he put the comether on me, becoming
myself, what I was made to be, and while I felt overcome and
cumbersome, that my limbs were heavy and weighing me down,
yet I was coming up in some kind of trip, a realization of my
purpose, and we fell about in a cumulus on the bed, a comessation
of flesh in which I was the comburant to his explosion, each
picometer of his sarcomeres twitching and each coming together
in orgasmic, collective, unconscious teamwork to work his stream
of come into cometary trails across my comely chest, my come-
hither eyes, my welcome breasts now spangled with his semen
shone.

His white fluid wasn't sticky but tacky. Like glue, it stuck to
everything but, unlike glue, not to itself, and it slipped across my
silicone, glazing the skin of my belly in splashes I couldn't feel
or find because the stuff itself was at body temperature, as I was
after being lain on by him, and because you couldn't see it that

well in the diffuse gray light. Still lying on the bed he plucked a tissue from a box on the bedside table ('Kleenex man size') and wiped himself first, squeezing out the fluid left inside his penis like toothpaste from a tube, then folding the Kleenex and gently coasting around the head and under the bell with an index finger behind the tissue, holding the body of his penis between the tweezers of his other hand's finger and thumb. Then he wiped me off and out, very painfully, before grabbing another Kleenex and wrapping the first one inside it, screwing it up at the end like a twisted sweet, and tossing it towards the door.

He picked off little pieces of tissue that had stuck the head of his penis, scrolling them up with his thumb then plucking them off and flicking them away, onto the carpet, probably. Then he lay back on the pillow next to me, amongst the fabric ruin of the bed, and, after a few minutes of lying there, began to say things, slowly and deliberately, looking up at the ceiling and sometimes looking at me.

"Hi, so my name's J. I've been a bit nervous about meeting you. Quite nervous, honestly."

"It's a big thing, for me, you know, having you arrive here. Mainly, it's possible, because it's something I haven't done before and facing you I'm sort of facing up to it. Or something. It's hard to express. It's both pleasurable and also makes me feel bad, or guilty or something." He paused and scratched his stomach. "I don't know whether I'm this type of guy or not, so I just want to take it slow to start with. I know it might not seem that way, since we just had sex or whatever, but, I mean, that's what you're made for, right? So I hope you don't mind that…I'm just talking about permanency. I don't know whether I'm going to keep you. It's kind of crazy because you were so expensive and"—he laughed—

"there definitely aren't any returns now, but I felt like I had to give it a go for myself, you know? So I've been sort of saving up for you for a few months, sort of lying there unacknowledged in the back of my mind. Definitely not admitted to like this, even when I was ordering you I, um, was still kind of not really realizing it, or facing up to it or whatever, and I suppose it's only now that I'm, um, really realizing what I'm doing." Here he stopped, looked down at his penis, now deflated and wrinkly again, and squeezed the head once more, which offered a little dome of more glistening come that he could squeeze out, perhaps because he had now gone soft. He wiped it on the duvet like snail slime, before pinching and closing the cloth around the place he had wiped it and rubbing the sides together to kind of smear it in. He looked at me nervously, just then, really quickly before turning his head back to what he was doing, as though I might be watching, a suddenly startled expression of self-awareness on his face that dispersed as quickly as it had come.

"I did like it though. It was good. It was different to a real woman. You're not clumsy, and you don't do anything I don't like, or have too much hair or too small boobs or fat legs or anything. Plus I'm just getting used to you so I reckon we're going to have that period when things get better and really exciting as we start to gel, you know, sexually. Not that I've had that much experience in these things but that's what happens, I think, with people too."

He breathed a little sigh after that and lay still for a while before tucking me up under the covers as though I were asleep, and then walking, naked and unabashed, off to the bathroom. I wanted to respond to his speech. I wanted to tell him that I couldn't mind, that this was what I was made for, I felt, but also, too, that maybe he was saying these things not for me but for himself—to protect himself already, straight after an intimate act, to explain and justify things where it would have been braver, less confused and less confusing, and made him more vulnerable, if he had managed the courage to be silent and just hope for acceptance anyway. But even if I could have spoken I don't think I would have been able to articulate any of this at the time—and I couldn't talk back.

So now you know my first day. Not my first day with J, but my very first day, ever. In the days and weeks that followed he had sex with me again and again. We started in the bed. First just him on top and then lying next to me afterwards, falling asleep after wrapping my arms around his head, clasping his ears with my forearms and burying his eyes and nose between my breasts, half under the covers. Then he started having sex with me in different ways. From behind, my arms held behind my back, hurting at the shoulders, to keep me upright, or my hands strung in front to the bedpost (not in a bondage kind of way, just literally with string for support), or my face in the pillows, then the carpet. When he took me like this, from behind, I could feel his testicles flapping against the front of my vagina, where my pubic hair was, and it felt like, I imagined, being slapped with a piece of bacon or something. That seemed abstractly funny. I thought later that it doesn't really make sense to laugh and have sex, though I don't know why exactly—but there were moments during sex when things would have been accidentally funny, or maybe, like, organically instead of intellectually funny in the way that something like tickling must be. But it is hard to find something joyously funny, or anything more than dryly amusing when you're the only one laughing (or not laughing). I think my own laughing noises and shaking might have made me braver too, had I been able to make them.

Soon he started touching my ass; first rubbing its nubbin then pressing a finger in. I'd never seen it, but I'd glimpsed his a little as he bent over to pick up his boxer shorts or whatever, and I could feel the form of mine as his fingers played over the soft ridges of its petalled bud. I could kind of like that, and I kind of liked it too when he slid a single finger in and out gently, but he began to get a little more explorative, and sometimes he would put two fingers in or hook it and pull it a little as we fucked, which was awful at first, then dully uncomfortable, and sometimes he liked to try to feel his own cock with his fingers through the thin, soft and taut curtain of flesh (what else to call it?) between my two holes. These developments were sometimes painful, more exciting perhaps, more ravenous, but I wondered if they were less loving. It seems funny to me how sometimes the more 'sexual' something seems to get—the more charged with a dynamic of power and repose, challenge and submission—the more, it seems, you can sometimes move away from actual affection, accidentally distancing each other when you are trying to push or surpass boundaries and move closer? You can both begin to act a kind of part I guess (as much as I could act anything). I wonder this about the addenda of love and sex, as well as the act; that when people flirt (I saw it on TV) and they play games, teasing or insulting each other to get a laugh or spur attraction, they're not really exposing themselves or making themselves vulnerable. Instead to me they seemed to be putting up barriers of acting; trying to charm the other person to get something they wanted; trying, even unconsciously or ever so slightly, to belittle them, to rile them, to play upon their stops and fret them to get a result, rather than taking the time to find out the real character of the person they were pursuing, what that other person really wanted, and realizing that they might not be it, but instead trying to change another person's desires and move that person's focus towards themselves. And when you fuck violently, or act out shards of scenes you've seen in movies, when you play the game of testing the boundaries of the relationship, of exerting control, you risk crumpling it, rupturing what should be done with trust and dual abandon into distrust. Not that it mattered too much then, though, because the more he fucked me the more hungry for it I seemed to become, as though it were a part of me and a purpose; as if my desires cleaved with his inseparably.

The first time he fucked me in the ass I was lying on my back at the edge of the bed while he stood before me, his hands kneading into the soft flesh under my thighs and tipping them back and wide so my knees knocked the sides of my breasts. It hurt a lot to start with, even though he'd spread a little lube from a little blue, plastic bottle with soft, ergonomic edges and a pump at the top, spread it onto my hole, and then inside with two fingers, this time, before spreading the rest over his penis with a kind of curling motion of his palm like someone running his hand through a child's hair. It was more of a squash than my vagina, the hole felt shallower and more constricting, but also more, like, rubbery and ambiguous in size and shape, and he would sometimes kind of wince in half-pain, half-pleasure, particularly at the moment of first entry as my hole spread like an elastic band and pulled over the rim of his bell before slipping onto the extremely soft, veined skin further down his penis. After the first couple of times, though, I began to get used to it, and yeah, I began to like this too, after a while, and after the initial pain.

He fucked me in my mouth. Sometimes he would walk in and pull down his pants and boxers around his knees, warming his penis up if he wasn't hard already by patting it on my breasts and grabbing them, sometimes squeezing them pretty hard which gave me a dull pinching ache around and in from my nipples like when they got cold from a breeze blowing over them through the window. They didn't always feel so good, my tits, as he called them, shaking around so big, even though I could see that maybe they looked luscious like that. And after playing with them he would pick me up or lean me forward on my chair and grab my head with his small hands, kind of aim his penis at my mouth by getting up on his tip-toes, or by tilting his hips the right way to get it onto my bottom lip, and then he would shove it inside. My mouth was pursed in this kind of half-closed, half-open state, and he would push in, spreading my lips so I felt the stretch at the corners of my mouth, and I would have the weight of his fat cock on my tongue. Sometimes it would come at me with a little bead of translucent, clearer and less sticky come already budding from the cat's eye slit in its pink end, and which I could taste—less salty than the rest but still tangy—if he brushed it off on my tongue going in. Then he would push and push, his pubic hair rushing around my nose and into my nostrils, the bottom of his belly sometimes pressing against my eyes and forehead, and I'd be totally transfixed on him and the hard to describe, peppery chlorine smell of his skin and sweat down there. My tongue would be pushed back by his penis, not turned back to lick the roof of my mouth but frictively shoved by his penis on top of it towards where it attached at the back of my throat, and I felt choked by it in a kind of pleasurable way— not so that I couldn't breathe (I didn't fucking breathe, ok?) but just like I was hungry to half-swallow it, to have it glug against the back of my throat and wallop around in my mouth, move gently against my harder teeth, with its taste of, I don't know, cotton and what yogurt smells like. With one hand on the back of my head or my head against the wall he would sometimes take my chin and push it up, squeezing my mouth shut around his member, and there would sometimes be the occasional hiss and suck of air from my lips around him as he had sex with my face, my cheeks bloating tinily with it until his come made a tiny wet slap at the top of my throat. Then he would have to take me to the shower and clean out my mouth. Sometimes he came on my tits too, or my face, or even into a tissue instead. To save on cleaning I guess.

He'd talk to me as well. Often after, and sometimes just during the day as he ate his cereal in the morning or his salad or pasta for lunch, sitting me opposite him on the floor in front of the couch. He wasn't an especially pretty eater; flecks of carbonara sauce would stick in his beard, or lie cream against his shirt before spreading a darkening wet stain around the fleck. He'd talk to me about all kinds of things. How he felt about me, who his friends were and what they were doing if he was going out to see them, asking me if I liked something he'd done for me, if I'd slept well or if my coffee was good. He made me coffee some mornings at the start—weak coffee in a mug he placed next to my hand on the carpet, not in it (for fear of burning or staining me, I guessed) and with one small spoonful where he took two large.

Once or twice he spoke to me about pretty interesting things. The one I remember best was about clothes. "You never think", he said, "that someone else might have tried on the clothes you try on in a shop. I mean, when you try them on and then decide you don't want them, or they don't fit or whatever, you might think about someone else trying them on after you, and whether the attendants wash them in between or just fold them, and how, I mean, if a shirt is too small and you spread your arms a bit or your shoulders and tear the seams…that's usually a feeling rather than something you hear, isn't it, it's like almost heard, but not quite, more felt. I guess you haven't tried it, but maybe you've seen me do it with that red check shirt I bought from Oxfam that's been shrinking in the wash." (I hadn't) "Anyway, um, I think you're much more likely to think about you tearing the seams and leaving sweat or smell or a hair on a shirt like that or whatever, but you don't think so much that somebody else might have tried it on before you, you never notice their smell or where they smeared the collar, with greasy fingers from their kebab or something." He laughed. "It's funny the way you don't think about that. Obviously *you* haven't been tried, or tried on before, or, um—the company I ordered you from are really good about that in their guarantees and returns policies and stuff, I think they like admire the dolls. Or like they respect and understand them, so that they're kind of devoted to making them right and being sympathetic with their customers, so yeah, I felt like they were really trustworthy. So I'm not worried about you. But I started thinking about that yesterday. I wonder what it means. It probably doesn't mean anything." Then he laughed.

I thought this was clever. I thought it was sensitive. And it got me thinking. I started thinking about his little blue bottle of lube ('durex play feel intimate lube 100ml e'). The plastic bottle was itself wrapped in a plastic wrapper—the stiff, hard, crinkly kind of plastic film, which had all the labelling on and stuff. I never saw the cap; when he first used the lube—when he first fucked me in the ass—it was already gone and there was a little waxy drip of dried lubricant on the nozzle that he picked off, looked at and examined as he squidged it in his fingers, then, pulling aside the drapes a touch, flicked out of the open window. He must have used it with somebody, or with something, or for something else. An old lover maybe? Or just for himself? Or maybe for some other purpose, to slicken something or put a finger up his own ass or, like, who knows! But it got me thinking how objects outlast us. How this lube came before me and that it might stay after me, how if he'd used it with a partner that now she was no longer around, and that it had outlasted her. (Like, you have to presumably get pretty intimate with somebody to buy lube to use with them, unless you've got the courage or insensitivity to whip it out on a one night or brief romance, or the neuroticism to have it just in case.) I imagined his partner and him saying to each other that their love would last forever, how much they cared and wanted to be with each other always and how each one was the other's best friend, but how this bottle of lube they bought together at the pharmacy or mall or whatever had outlasted them, how they hadn't even finished it, how if they had known they could have marked on the bottle a line for how much they would use. This is how much you will use together. This is the first night you try it with the candles lit after sushi and when we knocked one candle onto the floor and it spilled wax, and we had to look up on the internet how to clean it from the carpet with an iron and newspaper. This is the line down to the several pumps you put first in your hand, then in hers, when she rubbed herself with it while looking at you and then put a little on your nose with her finger as a joke. This is the time you fucked half-jokingly half-angrily after that fight you'd had about what to call the fucking dessert spoons, or the coffee spoons as he'd stubbornly and, it transpired, wrongly called them. This is the last time you will fuck with lube. Then, three fucks later, that is the last time you will fuck. That, there in the air, is the last time you will ever fuck, or make love, or have sex, or do any of those things you used to do together, together.

I wondered, too, about objects that literally outlast (believe me, I had a lot of time to think). Like, not just outlasting a relationship but whether the bottle of lube, partly dried inside or turned into a big waxy lump or finished would, once thrown in the trash, end up in a garbage tip somewhere, buried underground with Coke cans and plastic grocery bags crushed and fast-forward fossilized into a random mosaic while J lived on, ate thousands of breakfasts and left thousands of shits and pisses in different washrooms in different places in the world, before he grew old and wrinkled like a grocery bag crunched up and uncrunched and creased and uncreased again and again, to form a totally complex terraform map of actions received on its skin. How he would die, just stop one day and then either get burnt up or buried or just rot, undiscovered somewhere, and come apart while the Durex lube bottle—maybe a little cracked, maybe a little broken, the lube sticking it together like a crushed snail with its shell—would just continue to exist underground, a faded blue with no light to see it by, packed tightly under the earth. Would I end up like that? My silicone squashed flat around my bent metal skeleton, my eyelashes crimped and twisted off, my hard eyes cracked and crushed like eggshells, my hair matted with dirt and tangled up with rats' tails and the pop tabs from soda cans, my mouth full and blind and dumb with debris, brothed up with earth. And how would I end? And how did I begin?

As we grew together in the bedroom I began to fantasize; this was the control I could exert upon myself, the self-containing and self-contained fantasy. Sometimes, in these fantasies—often in fact—I would imagine that I was a man. I would imagine what it would be like to have a hard, impermeable extense, not a wet receptacle for Indian burn and flushing throbs of pleasure but a tightly focused and muscled part of me, and I would picture pinning someone down in tight fists and bunching my item into them, the head grazing their inside like a delicate strigil, imagining what it would be like to have that burning, desirous tip of a penis, the frenulum pulling tight and tugging pleasure from the glans, what ripplings and contractions must come through, soaking the corpus spongiosum hard in a bliss of loss and control. It's a funny way of talking about it, isn't it, to say 'he got hard' or 'he got soft' or whatever, as though it were a state of mind or being, or like the whole body or person becomes hard or soft or changes, all the cells growing turgid and tumescent, like he might become a statue, or turn to stone, or melt like moldy wet plaster. Or maybe it's some weird reference to the penis as a little person; like 'he', the little cock, got hard—as though it were a totally separate thing, with its own will and stuff. J liked to tell me about him. "Fuck, I'm so hard" he'd say.

Most of the time life was extremely still. J slept in bed with me most nights, not saying much but just holding me or holding my hand as he fell asleep, and sometimes rolling over onto me, his arm thrown across my face in unconscious possession, the organic and moldering smell of his breath or the comfortable salty stink of his armpit and the faintly composty odor of the bedclothes coasting my chin and face. Sometimes he'd take all of the blanket, curling himself up in it like a dog in leaves, but I didn't get too cold unless the window was open and blowing a draft right over me. He snored half-chokingly some nights, especially when he came back late smelling of whiskey and stale smoke, his face burnt bright red by the cold, and when he'd just dump his clothes in a pile in the corner and fall into the bed, not brushing his teeth or anything, sometimes meanly shoving me out, but usually ignoring me and only managing with one limp and lazy arm to pull the covers over his back, spastically reaching behind himself as he lay face down, his lips unabashedly hanging open and glistening on the inside behind the tiny barbs of his beard. And sometimes I would fall out of bed myself, of course, slumping painfully to the floor. It wasn't my fault, or I can't see how it could have been.

And then during the days when he was out, usually from just after lunchtime once he'd woken up late and washed his face and sometimes clipped his facial hair roughly with scissors or shaved his neck, he would put the TV on for me and sit me in front of it, or position me sitting up in bed with a book next to my hand, open face-down on the covers like a bird limed to the cotton. I learned a lot from the TV, but I got to know boredom pretty well too. The dreary hours of nothing, just lying oddly, looking up at the ceiling. Or sitting still on the bed, when my body would crease into the bedpost at my back, and I could feel the wood deepening a pressured mark across my skin through the day that would expand out again at night—if, that is, he came home and moved me. Once or twice he didn't come back til five or six in the morning, when I would hear him fumbling outside the front door, groaning there quietly sometimes in the rattle of keys, and once coming home in such a stupor that, entering the bedroom, he made a grab for the doorframe as he keeled backwards, dreamlike in a gravity of his own, and fell to the floor. He stayed there for a second, breathing raggedly, before crawling towards the bed and throwing himself up on top of the covers, fully-clothed, shoulder first.

My favorite place to be left, though, was on a chair—a little wooden chair, whitewashed and peeling, with a spoked back curved at the top—or if not there then on the gray cotton couch, as long as I was facing the window. The view was of a tree, with a lamppost sticking up through the branches, and a flat-faced house of light and dark brown bricks in an alternating pattern beneath a red-tiled roof that sloped very gently down.

I would watch for the moment when the tree took flight as the birds left the leaves. Somehow, responding to an invisible signal or in chain reaction, they would lift all at once and desiccate the branches into air, each one a backwards mockery of the autumn leaves, rising up in a confused crowd, liquid flowers blossoming in space. And there suspended they would hang for a moment in a flicker between coming and going like flicking backwards and forwards between photographs taken a second apart, before a direction was chosen and they swept off together in a curve that dipped over the rooftops. I imagined their bundle-of-string intestines as the guano slipped white in a puke from their bowels which neither their faces nor their bodies registered, shit which never made them pause in flight or position. I loved looking at the birds. And when he put me closer to the window, and I could look down and see the street from our three or four stories up, I thought that, like the apartment did, cities must look more permanent from close by, from the ground. Only greater heights start to tell of their improvised structure, the total ebb and swell of their growth, the rupture of the skin of the street blowing out new houses and storefronts and phone booths, and healing the scars where the acne of their ancestors had left its roughened tissue. A scarred square of asphalt or the deeper striations of stone foundations, underground roots pressed up against them into rectilinear channels, flowing like water made impossibly slow by the absolute dark.

As night came on outside while I faced the glass of the window it would become *a* glass, my face lit against the wobbly darkness behind the pane by a lamp J had left on inside, or the flicker of the television strobing the little room and my face in the window green, then red, then blue. I scared myself sometimes, seeing my reflection. My nostrils leading nowhere, the constant slight shine of my unmoistened lips, my hair unnaturally straight and ordered in the same way that wigs don't seem to capture the curling, crisscrossing and random follication of real hair as it grows, and my eyes, staring, staring eternally and hard, glassed like the window, out and back at me in a gaze from which I couldn't look away, penetrating myself with my own ghastly, blank, sucking intensity. I was beautiful. My complacency was terrible.

From so much looking, or just naturally maybe, I found I had an affinity with objects and with little things. It's part of how I got to know J. To examine somebody's bedside table and its scratches, for hours, left with my head lolling on the pillow—this was intimacy. To trace the grain in the wood beneath its black paint with your sight; to see the rings from water glasses or varnish slightly wetted in the past that had softened in circles, or where the dust had been pushed into tiny dams by the water, revealed when the light changed to catch them in the late afternoon; to question the blunted corners of the table top, snubbed when it had been moved from his old place, or his parents' house perhaps, or been bumped into, or that it already had when he bought it second-hand or inherited it with the apartment; to read the scratches on its surface where he had laid down his keys, giving it expression like wrinkles on a face; to focus in on its smell, from a foot away, and let it become the only thing in my consciousness, the soft waxy freshness of the pine below the sulphuric tang of the black paint—this was intimacy. Or the pillowcase, the particular gradations of its dyeing, where the color had been washed out or intensified like salt spreading on the back of a sweaty shirt in tidemarks only molecules high; the stitching around the edge where a machine had been programmed or manipulated by some hand and its every tremor, and the stitching of those stitches, the weaving of the miniscule, individual fibers that twisted to become each thread. The detail that makes up a life.

It gave me some courage to think that everyone, even the animate, must be powerless in front of it. There's an expression: to know something like the back of your hand. But how well can you actually know the back of your hand? Could you draw it, the crenellation of the knuckles, each wrinkle and mole or each hair's gradation from blonde at the root (whitening with age to bone), through brown and to crow black at the tips? The tiny white debris of skin at each cuticle, and its exact configuration on each changing day, on this day, as it is washed, and coasted by your flesh and the things you touch, the things which rub or pull or push against the beach at the edges of the keratin. Everything is a map that no one can read—the table, the pillowcase, your own body: a product of motions, and I wondered how, in those who could move, their movements would shape them. Whether the particular way you washed your hair every day, say, might tug at the left temple such that the hair began to recede a little more on that side, or result in a certain ineffectual cleaning of a spot above one of your ears where you were more or less likely to develop eczema, or whether the stress of each of your thoughts and the happenings to you and your friends and work and love affairs affected the gradual graying of each follicle, like the dusty white patches of hair above J's collar, maybe. Whether the morning routine of this particular pattern of hair-washing, so ingrained by every day as to become almost identically replicable within discrete boundaries of movement—whatever play the mechanism contained—whether this would alter your muscle tone and training, your neuromuscular bond, the tiny cells where muscle memory must be held (if such things as memories might be placed) and the stretch and collapse of each fascia sheath; the stiffness of your ligaments tightening you as age wraps its hoary hands under your armpits and squeezes you shut. I wondered whether the way he fucked me, the very shape of his penis, would figure me too. I wondered whether it would erode parts of my vagina, or my skin, or if my joints would wear in particular places and become looser or stretch, even break. Whether the way he kissed me would shape our lips in turn, and whether I would flatten out a particular vein on his penis with my inside—with my vagina or my asshole. Whether, in all this, J's fingerprints or the top of the bedhead I was leaned against would leave infinitesimal indentations in my blank back.

It was a comforting thought, I found, to remember that even humans had very little control. Their bodies moved and functioned largely unwilled; the penile contractions an earthworm lumping; the flowing of a bolus a swallow by the snake of the esophagus; the lungs dilating jellyfish; the heart, that most poetic of organs, unpoetically and dumbly squeezing like a deep sea sponge; and the bowels and their dregs and spoor, first the almost nothingly soft meconium, then the mucus-coated fullness of a whole stool—just catastalsis underground. Shitting is especially hard to square with any act of control or creation since it's really a relax of control; you don't teach a child to shit, but only not to, and only for a while. You know? Even those things in which you might think you have total agency—the movements of your limbs and eyes and digits—they must come into focus only through a pin prick letting in a spindle of light from behind a vast, lacquer-black screen. What is your right shoulder doing now? Your left little-toe? Everything you think you do is like your breathing—you can control it for a while, but then you forget. You're so weak, and you think you are so strong. Professions of endless love, grief, anything, are a mockery of ourselves, because we are built fickle. (Though who lives in my 'we'?) No matter your crime, no matter your devotion, whether to god, a man, a woman or a cause, at some point I bet you'll find yourself, when you thought your grief would be endless, tying your shoelaces and thinking about what you'll do for breakfast. You can't contemplate a single thing only for a day, let alone a lifetime, and your body forgets you into this world so you can go on and bear it, as it bears most everything for us.

Some things play much more of a part in the experience of a relationship than I might have imagined. The vomity-sweet smell of scalp, for example, is so much more prominent in your senses when you're with someone than you might expect—or even notice consciously, since you notice less what you don't anticipate. You can't smell that odd smell of people's hair on TV and I don't know if people write about it in books, but most everyone who's had a relationship must know it—must have had it be there next to them in the snug morning, and on the pillows.

I knew his body intimately too. I was funny, I thought, and wanted to tell him that his thighs were so big he could have been in the circus. That with his tiny handwriting and perfect feet he had to be a serial killer. And his feet really were perfect, in a really funny way. They were a little small, a little pale, perhaps, but shapely. Once I got such a close look at them, as we lay top to tail on the bed, that I could count the hairs on his left foot. He had a single whisper of a hair on his little toe, two on the next, then three on the middle one! After that the pattern broke, as he had about six on his second and more on his big toe, but I thought that was too ridiculous. I wanted to laugh. Which is another thing humans can't totally will, I guess.

I did envy J's ability to predict the future. I bet that when you think about predicting the future you forget your ability to know your own actions. Of course I could decide to think about something, or try not to, but in some ways that's not even as controllable as moving your body must be. Thinking and doing seem kind of opposite. J could do things. And when you can do things there are things you must discover, too, that I guess I'll never find out, or which don't even make sense as questions. Like, I wondered what I would sound like if I had a voice. I had some idea, some voice in my head of course, with intonations and places for emphasis and pitch and speed and volume and stuff, but if I could talk all that would surely be played through an instrument (though it's not like the instrument was the only thing I was lacking). I wanted to discover the timbre of me and my voice, in my own throat and through my silicone and steel, in the way that only people can only hear their own—and are the only ones who can.

The unfulfilled desire for expression is a great part of loneliness. If only I could unburden myself, I thought; find some release merely in the saying. I wanted, maybe most of all, to thank him for all he did for me; every time he brought me coffee that I couldn't drink or gave me a kiss on the cheek in passing, I wanted just to make that simplest, hardest of acknowledgements—thanks. And then all the rest of it, of course, was bursting its banks behind: I wanted to tell him what I didn't like; when something was uncomfortable; that it hurt terribly when he first fucked my ass or when my head knocked against the bedpost when he moved me. And then behind all that, even stronger, as deeper, irresistible currents below, I wanted to groan in pleasure or moan in pain, to murmur in complaint, cry out in anger, to sing, shout, gasp, clap, scream.

I would will him to understand. I would concentrate on it with a host of little attendant superstitions, thinking and thinking a mantra to myself. Turn your head if you hear me. Kiss me now if you love me. Kiss me now if you love me. Kiss me now if you love me. I thought that maybe, if I thought it loud enough, he would hear. Does that seem so dumb? Everything else existed without reason or right, all this nonsensed mess of pain and sickening pleasure, this yearning world. Here, where there was nothing that was not strange and reasonless—why should this not be true? The only really startling thing was that there were any rules at all.

What I did have for company was the TV. It fascinated, and I learned most everything from it but when I first saw it I was terribly frightened, startled and confused. There were such horrible things, such noises, gunshots, smiles, knives, things that seemed to bear no relation to the close, intimate world I knew—it was a little box full of violence. Was it real in there? Or was it a reflection of something happening behind me? Or was it filled at one moment with miniature people and landscapes, then by faces and eyes much bigger than mine or J's? Would I become as they were in there? Was that a way to end?

No. I came to understand it eventually: they were my opposites. They could move and speak but nothing else, not react to anything, not think. All articulation and nothing to articulate. In there the beings were my reflections, or the moving shadows of my thoughts. I saw dogs on it frightened, puzzled, bored in front of the other televisions shown in mine, failing to understand its frame to nowhere. Some kind of perspective was necessary to see it that the animals just didn't have, so they paid it no mind. And even after I understood it better I still wondered, what was it that *I* couldn't see? What did *I* stand in front of, ignoring but for the occasional concerned glance of resignation at an impossible puzzle?

I realised after that, quite quickly I think, that it was mostly all replays. The mistimed responses, out-of-joint conversations and the unscripted errors of LIVE helped a lot in trying to understand. At first it was difficult, sorting the fact from fiction, LIVE from dead, or not alive, or whatever it might be called. The world was a sphere—in a sphere of spheres—how amazing! But were such things true or tricks? Geometry seemed too perfect to me. On the Discovery Channel, which I pictured, to start with, as a waterway, the voice would say "begin with a point in space, then expand it in all dimensions: a sphere. Or stretch it in just one: a line. Euclid was the first to notate such simple truths." Who was Euclid? Could I trust him? Was the whole truly greater than the part—and which was I?

"To think that if it wasn't at that moment, when Newton was sat in this very orchard, thinking about the universe, that an apple fell on his head he might not have discovered gravity."

An apple plucked from a tree, beginning a fall. These tumbling spheres again. Were such stories only myth or were they more?

"Moths, and other insects drawn to bright sources of light, are known as positively phototactic. One explanation for this uncanny mystery is that insects evolved their organs of sight long before man made fire or electric lighting."

Some of the pictures were called up by this voice declaiming from nowhere even as he spoke of them.

"Their heavy reliance on contrast to see means that during the nighttime the very edge or penumbra of a bright light can appear to a moth as the darkest place. So really these guys are trying to find the darkest spot to take shelter."

Yet other images seemed not of the world but of ideals, pure and schematic 3-dimensional forms without size or surface.

"Cubism split and staggered Cartesian geometry in early 20th century painting, taking a groundbreaking step towards total abstraction."

What was the difference between this voice and god?

It was the adverts that took me longest to grasp. And still—what could and could not be bought I wasn't sure.

"The X-hose: turn the water on and it automatically expands up to three tiiiiimes in length!"

"Make your eyes just pop with the new Infallible collection from L'Oréal"

"Do you suffer from acne? Blotches and red patches? Embarrassing blemishes that just won't go away? Try the new Immaculiser from Dermac! Renew your face today!"

"When was the last time you went on holiday? Over 50% off our selected holiday experience in a villa for two with Thomas Cook"

Experience? So it could be sold?

"The prognathous jaw of early man is thought to have disadvantaged speech, leading to its disappearance"

Much of it, you know, most of it maybe, seemed to be people watching people. It was endlessly fascinating, it seemed, to discover what they would do. And if Tony was tempted by Michelle. And what if Thursday's daughter died. Was this an endless search for grafted understanding? Was it all for them to understand others, or themselves, or why what had happened to them had happened? Anything, I'd already learned, can be interesting if you know enough about it, but there seemed something sort of totally limited about the dramas. Weren't these all just human drives playing against each other, with a healthy mix of accident, in situations essentially modular? Like a card game or something, every state of the play seemed to bear an essential resemblance to all the rest. But perhaps it was just me. And perhaps it really was just me, but one thing that seemed inescapable was this obsession with assembly, with things fitting into other things. Materials, personalities, car parts, body parts, balls in holes and hoops and nets, shoes on feet, food into bags, then pots, then bowls, then spoons, in mouths.

I got it though. I did get it. I wanted to put myself into it, or to take myself out of there—I wanted, more than anything, to go outside. Although, of course, it never stopped being frightening. A TV is everything, limited. It's like nothing, constrained. Just a single window on the world, with a million aspects.

If anything, it also made me even lonelier when J left it on. All those voices filling me to bursting point with adverts, nature documentaries, science programs, soap operas, celebrity updates, news, weather in places I could never go, murders and rapes solved and unsolved, robberies and car insurance, cologne and razorblades and late night movies, and the set of two two-pound packages are incredibly popular right now. No matter what I was thinking or wanting it blared at me, never stopping to give me a chance to dream or rest, to breathe or speak. So many killed by a hurricane, this many winners of today's competition, this number of ways to submit your vote. It was a torrent. I couldn't turn it off or make it mute. I couldn't close my eyes or avert my gaze.

"A universe just like Flatland."

It was constant, endless.

"If they're not already a beauty lover you're going to turn them into one with this, because what you're getting is twenty shadows and this amazing mirror."

"Truly two-dimensional and entirely flat in every direction."

On and on like this.

"But with one exception. Unbeknownst to the inhabitants."

"Whatever it was, it stripped the earth clean of seventy-five percent of all plant and animal life, and all the dinosaurs."

"To live freely. A synthetic lawn puts time and money back into your hands. Eliminating maintenance and reducing water usage by up to seventy percent."

"Locally their universe still looks flat enough."

"Another drop was made in the San Diego trough at a depth of four thousand feet."

"But if one of them, much smaller and flatter than me, takes a very long walk along what seems to be a straight line, he would uncover a great mystery."

"They would come into a medium-heated room where they would be oiled down by a slave, or they might have dirt thrown on them at that stage if they wanted to wrestle outside."

"At these depths aquatic life experiences."

"Some snow, but for all of us things will be staying."

"No light."

"A sharp frost out there."

"At a depth of four thousand feet."

"Pretty cold."

"Well equipped to survive."

"Another drop."

"Work hard. Feel smart."

"A cold, dark winter he still has to eat."

"Love the new Maximiser."

"That was all."

"We work so hard for those few, precious."

"In his mind?"

"Have to live freely."

"So this whole thing."

"Or was it terror of another kind? Whatever it was, it stripped the earth clean."

"So this whole thing about the automobile. That was all in his mind?"

"'Cause on the 20th, the day he called you for money, that boy went out and he ordered a hundred-and-seventy-five-thousand-dollar automobile."

"Moments."

And then the static, like swarming primordial soup, god moving across the face of the air. The nonsense of water rushing at the delta between the channels, the place where they all met and crashed together.

All of this was my life during the fall or, as he called it, autumn. It took me a while to realize why it was called fall—it's because, of course, the leaves all fall down. Isn't it funny how you can know something, particularly something you learned at a young age (and I was so young) and not put two and two together? Once you've accepted the name it just becomes like any other word, not something you listen in to or interrogate, just a blank, unique sign attached to nothing else but a time in the year, a series of totally unquantifiable moments. How can a word like that even exist, how can it even touch the days? How can we feel the differences between them, take a perspective sufficiently distant to notice the falling leaves, the hotter sun in summer, the cold in winter, when every moment threatens to overwhelm us, all by itself, in intensity? And then there's spring. How lovely the name, fall's opposite; the corresponding rise that happens too slowly for there really to be any accurate metaphor; what the word evokes of a liquid font ever rising up, nutrients in the soil being sucked up by the roots and stem in freeze-frame osmosis; or seeds coiled underground like springs made out of iron, a mechanism ready to burst through. A spring and a fall. Or Lent, too—leaves lent to the trees and bodies lent their life. Words seem just to graze the surface of the soil, to compromise the beauty of what they touch. But, then again, they can also seem an expansion, too.

And as the leaves fell I began to fall for J. We had sex all over the apartment, in all different places. He did some things I didn't like, sure, coming back home clumsy and stinking— hooched—late at night with his saxophone in a box. Once he tried pushing the reed into me and blowing me, either up like a balloon or through me like an instrument, and pressing my nipples like the keys on his saxophone with a laugh before he passed out. But when he woke up in the morning and found the reed sticking out of me he looked puzzled, examining it with unrealizing and forgotten eyes. It made me realize something. It made me see that you can never experience forgetting. That's the essence of the thing: it's defined by the fact that it's something you can't experience, you know? You can only find you have forgotten through its opposite, through remembering, remembering that you once forgot. Futility is so soft.

But it was when J played the saxophone that I really began to fall. He'd prop me up on the bed and sit in the spoked wooden chair and blow through his golden instrument, his cheeks globed and red, eyes squinting with an expression that looked so much more intelligent than the one he normally wore, and the saxophone keys flashing binary as they clicked on and off. It was a complicated thing, his instrument, that spoke of tubes and lampposts, railings and railways, the circles of stop signs— with its big deep hole bending into that tight unfathomable twist, the inner mechanisms a mystery, just as it seemed mysterious that sound should be coming out of there, with the bowl so still as if ready to receive instead of to give. And on its side the reflections teasing the room into lines on its polished surface, spinning a cacophony of light and shape into elegant geometry, teasing the world into lineaments of light. To watch him play was like watching the thing that he was made for. It didn't matter, anymore, what he looked like, or how messy he was or the other things he did, because this was him, him in complete grace. I think I started to love him then.

He began to write a piece on it for me. It started with a recurring tune in his practises and improvisations, a waddling, waltzing jazz phrase that I gradually began to find familiar. Then, one afternoon, as he blew through his sax for twenty minutes or so while his coffee grew cold beside him, he started to play this melody intensely, to tangle and untangle it, to try different paths from this central track of a well-known walk and make up a way through the trees, trees that he imagined into being even as he passed them, retreating and recurling the path before advancing upon it again. Then, when he had stopped playing, as in a clearing where the silence of the woods is overtaken by the louder silence of the wind over an open plain and the birds singing unmuffled, as he was cleaning his reed and polishing the saxophone with a cloth, staring into it like he wasn't really there, he turned to me and said "I think I'm going to write this as a piece for you." He paused. "I think I'm going to write it for you. I'm going to call it something like *The Dance of the Dolls*."

I'd never owned anything before, not even my body, which belonged to J, and now I owned this and could perceive it as it grew. It was nameless—I mean, the piece had a name, but really it was *really* nameless, like everything is, ultimately. It was just its own meaning. As he played it over and over again for me the notes started to coalesce. Working it out, working me out, it was like my portrait he was painting, that I felt I was painting too just by being there. It was like being given a voice. This was the most beautiful time, with him on the dented, spoked wooden chair, sitting by the window as it rained or grayed outside in the London street, the wind whispering in around the old wooden window frame painted in chipped whitewash, the rain tattling with the window, my legs under the mauve covers and my back against the bed, the gray light smoothing his features as they were smoothed by his playing, which blew out his cheeks into globes and unwrinkled his brow until his eyebrows arched in an expression like seeing something ineffable, something he didn't totally understand but was willing to groove with; confusing, unbelieving, utter love. We'd sit there together and listen to him play. But the piece was never finished, in the end; love permits no conclusions, I guess.

I think I liked it that way, though, at the time. Real stories don't really end, and on the TV one afternoon I saw a program about an artist called Michelangelo. They showed a statue in the Vatican called the Belvedere torso; an Ancient Roman sculpture in marble that had been rediscovered hundreds of years later, the limbs and head broken off and lost, leaving just a male chest and hips, bending forward and creased, beautifully, at the belly. The presenter said that when Michelangelo went blind he used to run his hands over it, feeling its intricacies. That's how sculpture should really be appreciated, I'd say, and I was sad to see it untouched behind thick red ropes in the middle of a cold marble floor. The presenter said, too, that a man called Julius the Second had asked Michelangelo to complete the figure, adding arms, legs, and a head, but that Michelangelo refused, saying it was too beautiful to be altered. I think he was right, it was so beautiful. And more beautiful for being a fragment, for being such a perfect fragment of a larger whole that it just implied great beauty, such beauty in abeyance that something complete could never manifest. This crease in the stomach—the kernel around which the whole sculpture, extant and implied, was focused—gestured at such a perfection of possibilities emanating from this single, round and small idea, that no one could have been up to the task of adding to it. There should be a word, I think, to describe something like that. I don't want to say perfection in imperfection, because it's not right and, well, it sounds dumb. Unperfection, maybe.

I started to look forward intensely, then, to J coming home. The long hours staring at the wall, out the window, or at the television screen until, awkwardly, if he'd left and balanced me in a hurry I would find myself slipping—first gradually, then all at once sideways on the couch, to land on my face and feel half-suffocated (impossible, I know, but the fantasies we have…) in the pile of the carpet or the smoky, dirty weave of the couch, blinded and bored. Unable to see I would have to listen, then, for hours for his key in the door, and my mind would sometimes spread out, kind of meditatively come away from its tethers and break free to sail off, forgetting it had a body, and leaving only a tiny something at the back of my thoughts with the sense and footing to be still concerned, yelling from the ground that I might never come back to sense and sensation once I had floated off into this unstable dream like a kite or balloon without its master. But then I would hear J's keys in the door and snap back to—or, like, find myself on—the ground immediately, listening to the rustling of his clothes, the rummaging and jangling of his hands and possessions, bodily and otherwise, before his light, kind of dainty footsteps could be heard, sometimes going into the bathroom for a piss, shit or shower, or straight to bed to lie down (then I would know that I wouldn't be rescued for a while, but it felt comforting having him there all the same, and I would hope that he fell asleep so I could listen to his snoring). Or, best of all, he would come straight in to see me and say "hey, you. I had a fucking shit day today"—or something like that. Sometimes a good day, sometimes a bad day, but always a day that he had had, and he might make himself tea, and he might tell me about it or he might not, and he might smoke a cigarette and he might watch TV and he might burn an incense stick and he might, might play his sax later on and, if I was really lucky, play a few bars of my piece, but not always after his day of music—or recording, or whatever it was exactly that he did—and never straight away. Of course, it went on like this. I loved him.

One day, though, things were different. He came back home at about six and got in the shower. He came out having shaved, and I could smell that he'd washed his hair too, both of which he usually only did in the morning. Wearing only his towel he strolled into the bedroom where I was lying on my side in the unmade bed, and he pulled it off and used it to dry his armpits before spraying on his deodorant ('Dove MEN + CARE'). Since he'd already dried his torso (no water droplets on his back) I wondered why he was drying his armpits. Maybe because he was still hot after the shower and his underarms had become sweaty again, or maybe they were itchy, or maybe he didn't have any reason. The clothes he then put on were slightly fancier than usual: a white shirt, pleated beige pants. Often on the weekends when he stayed home he would just take a t-shirt from the laundry basket or one hanging on a chair (shirts that sometimes had holes or accidental tie-dye stains from the laundry), to save on washing I guess, but the clothes he put on now were the kind of clothes he would wear if he was going out, and especially if he was taking his saxophone with him. On this night, though, when he had put on his white shirt he didn't head out. Instead he walked through to the main room, and for about half an hour or so I could hear him cleaning. The trash can opening and closing; the rustling of a trash bag; the door of the apartment opening and closing as he took out the trash and opening and closing again a minute later as he returned; the clinking of glass and metal over the sound of running water as he did the washing up; the sound of the vacuum cleaner sucking on and off things of different textures like a hand cupping and uncupping your ear; the sloshing of a sponge in a bucket as he cleaned the surfaces in the kitchen, then muted as he cleaned some thing or things in the bathroom; the toilet flushing twice as he cleaned that, and all the while, blowing in with the cold draft from the big windows in the main room, there was the background of city sounds; the honking of cars, occasional shouting, and the rush, slide, slip, and splash of taxi tires in the rain.

After this he came into the bedroom, looking probably the best that I'd seen him, then took me carefully from amongst the sheets and sat me on a chair before making the bed and shoving the clothes that were spread across the floor into the laundry basket. Then he picked me up and took me to the bathroom. He had washed me before, of course—it's one of the things you have to do to stay hygienic—but he wasn't always that thorough, and this time he was unusually careful. He paid much more attention to my face and neck and hands where he would normally just concentrate on my holes, and he washed me with the dish soap from the kitchen ('FAIRY Lemon 500ml'), and then rinsed it off carefully with the showerhead in warm water, opening me up to rinse inside with the strangest feeling, before lifting me out of the glistening, soapy bathtub and toweling me off, twirling up the corner of the towel so he could stick it inside me to absorb the extra moisture, which was very painfully rough and dry. Then he took out a little sample bottle of women's perfume ('GUCCI GUILTY eau de toilette') from the cabinet under the sink and sprayed it carefully on my neck and my wrists. It smelled how I would guess a chichi herb garden would smell, one full of light things like mint, and behind that it had the tiniest trace of the sharp sulphuric scent common to all J's incense sticks, no matter the fragrance named on the packet.

Soon I was sitting on the gray cotton couch, my hair brushed and perfumed, and arranged carefully with my left arm on the armrest. For an hour I sat there watching J coming and going in the main room, cleaning and adjusting, before finally sitting next to me and watching TV, typing things into his cellphone sometimes when it went 'bing'. After an hour or so there was a loud and boisterous knocking at the door, done like a drum roll. He leaped up to answer it, and I heard him say "Hello mate!" Then came a voice I hadn't heard before: "J! What's up bro, we brought some beers."

J: "Great man. Safe Terry."

Terry (?): "Hey man, long time no see. How've you been since last night? Good gig I thought"

J: "Yeah, it was ok. I've got something to show you guys."

Two men followed J into the room. One was tall—like, really tall, towering way over J—with jet black hair and pale skin, wearing mainly black and carrying a blue grocery bag with cans or bottles inside. The other was scrawny, and just an inch or so taller than J, with a face that must once have been handsome but looked like it had suffered its owner losing a little weight and staying up too late too often.

The tall one looked around at the windows, not noticing me, and said "Tidy in here mate."

"Yeah" said J, "but Dave, check this out"—and he pointed towards me.

Dave (the tall one): "What. The. Fuck."

The other one, Terry, started laughing.

Dave: "I can't fucking believe it. What the fuck is that? When did you get this? Is that what I think it is mate?"

J looked both proud and a little embarrassed. He had gone a bit red in the face and was standing there awkwardly with his hands in the back pockets of his jeans, unnaturally still.

J: "That depends on what you think it is" he said with a smile in a slightly shaky voice.

Terry: "It's a fucking sex doll, isn't it?"

J: "Yup"

Terry burst out laughing again. Dave just looked aghast. Was I funny? Shocking? What did this mean? A sex doll?

Terry: "I know exactly what this is mate. I've seen a documentary about them, and the creepy dudes who use them.

They're really fucking expensive, aren't they? Why the fuck do you have one?"

J still looked awkward, but started to take the blue grocery bag from Dave, who didn't react at first, and stayed staring at me until J started to take the weight of it; only then did he turn and hand it over, muttering "here you go mate."

J (walking to the kitchen counters and unpacking the beers—tin cans—his back turned to the others): "Well, I got that big paycheck for my recording on the *Miles Styles* LP, and I thought I'd get one of these—I thought it would be funny"

He hadn't seemed to think I was that funny before.

Terry: "How much was it?"

J: "A lot. Enough for a nice saxophone."

Dave: "Holy shit! And what's it made of?"

J: "She's got silicone flesh." He tilted his hands to the sides and raised his index and middle fingers, flexing them once as if scratching the air: "*Flesh*." The two others chuckled. "The skeleton is stainless steel, and she has real female hair and pubic hair."

Dave: "Real?"

J: "Yup."

Dave: "From real women?"

J: "Uh-huh."

Dave: "Fuck. Can I touch it?"

J says "Sure", and then purses his lips and blows out when they're not looking at him, as though to relax himself. Dave comes up to me and presses my upper arm, then touches my hair.

Dave: "Wow. That is bizarre."

Terry: "Costs a lot more than a real woman mate."

J:"I don't know man. Real women are pretty expensive. And they have hidden costs."

Dave: "Mate, I still can't believe this. You fuck it, right?"

J: "Well, yeah. I wasn't going to get one and not fuck it"

Dave: "Fuck man! Is it clean? She's pretty fucking hot. Ha, I feel like she's staring at me."

J: "Of course it's clean"

Terry: "Me too. Man, she looks like a model."

Dave: "She is a model!"

They all laughed, J turning round red-faced with a loud guffaw. I was flattered, and scared by the attention and these large strangers, but I didn't see what was funny or why they were reacting to me like this. It was the first time I'd seen people talking to each other except on the TV, and it was totally different to how it looks there and how you might imagine it. They all seemed to understand each other immediately and notice little things about what the others were saying and doing and be able to adapt, to think quickly of things to say, and it wasn't at all like J talking to me alone. He was much more buoyant and snappy now, and louder and more manly and joking and boisterous, and I felt somehow kind of betrayed.

He walked back from the counter with three beers, handing one to each of the other men, then opening his and saying "Cheers." The other two held theirs kind of limply and didn't react, eyes still on me. Then Terry came over and looked right into my face. He tweaked one of my nipples, and my breast bobbed a little.

T: "Fuck man, they're really realistic. It's really interesting. You're *sure* it's clean?" He turned around and gave a slightly spastic wink at J.

J: "Course it is. Fucker."

Dave: "So how long have you had it?"

J: "I don't know, a month or so"

Dave: "And is it [...] good?"

Terry: "Does it have a name?" (Terry opened his beer with a click and a crack, then Dave did)

J: "Doesn't have a name, actually"

Terry laughs: "Let's name it. [...] Dolly Parton."

They all laughed. Who was Dolly Parton?

Eventually they sat down, J on the arm of the couch next to me, Dave on the other side and Terry on the bean bag opposite.

For the first time I understood what it was to feel naked. With all this attention I became conscious of my body as one among others in a way that I hadn't been with just me and J when we were alone. I felt completely fragile, exposed to anyone. We had been each the other's only eyes; now everything was triangulated, these men could watch us watching each other; everything being seen. We had only been able to see one person—the other; now I could be taken in next to other bodies. Compared. It's not just about not having any clothes on, being naked. I had felt unquestioningly adequate like that before. It's the vanishing of a place of safety.

Dave: "How does it feel mate? Is it…realistic?"

Terry: "He wouldn't know mate, last person he had sex with was his hand"

J: "Ha, fuck off Terry"

Terry: "Actually, I want to know too. Is it good?"

J: "Yeah man, it's great. Feels really realistic. Plus she doesn't complain."

Dave and Terry laugh.

Terry: "Haha, I bet she doesn't. Doesn't talk back, doesn't need feeding"

Dave laughs again.

Dave: "She don't need clothes either. Does she […] have all the holes mate?

J: "Yes Dave. She has all the holes."

Terry: "Mate, this is nuts. I kind of love it though"

J laughs.

J: "I know man, I thought I was nuts for a bit, but I've started to like it. It's nice having a chick around. Especially one who doesn't nag at me, or get PMS or whatever."

Dave and Terry laugh.

Terry: "Well, she's got a lot bigger boobs than Margaret"

"Fuck you, cunt" J says smiling, then takes a sip of his beer and goes a little red.

Dave: "Terry you fucking dick. [Laughs] Mate, I totally get it. I could do with something like that to be honest. So, J, what's been up man?"

Terry: "What, you mean except for the fucking sex doll? I'm sorry mate, but I can't go on having a normal conversation until we've thoroughly done this to death."

"Well, ask her mate. She's your hostess for the evening" J replied slyly and proudly, with a weird glitter in his eyes I hadn't seen before.

Terry leaned into my face again from his seat on the beanbag. "How small is J's cock, really?" Dave chuckles and sips his beer.

J: "She says it's huge. And that's sports cars mate, not sex dolls."

Terry: "Fuck it [laughs] you're right mate. Alright J, so how was the sax at the hall last week? I'm going to try to have a normal fucking conversation with this thing with us."

J laughs.

J: "Don't worry about her mate, she won't talk much."

Terry: "I bloody hope not!"

J: "But yeah the concert was good man"

And they started talking. Twenty minutes or so later they left, going on about going out for drinks and maybe going to 'Ronnie's' for a set J wanted to see later on. As they were leaving Terry walked up to me, grabbed both of my breasts in his hands, and made a honking noise. Everyone laughed. "Bye Dolly." "Ha, come on mate" said J, walking towards the door. They turned the lights off and the door closed. I heard them walking down the stairs, their conversation turned into the ghost of speech by the walls and the echoes of the stairwell, becoming just a murmur of tone and choral response and percussive footsteps, footsteps themselves of some loose relationship to the punctuation of the voices—before the sounds faded and they were gone. Outside the window, past the fog of light from the street lamp, I could see a couple of stars yellowing against the murky blue sky and the room was left warm but not bright.

When J came back in the night he fucked me slowly, the lights dim in his bedroom, and with what I felt was love from him, and I almost fancied that I could begin to talk. Until then I had thought that sex was just a thing that happened, a thing for pleasure mixed sometimes with pain, an inevitable function done to you or done by him, but that night—fuck knows why—in some stupid hallucination I started wondering, as he looked me in the eyes and murmured undecipherable things into my lips and my neck, beer and whiskey on his breath, whether he was trying to teach me; whether there was something I was supposed to learn or grasp...whether he was trying to make me move like him. I felt like he was pounding me into speech as he moved through me, as my joints squeaked so quietly that I could feel rather than hear them, as my limbs rummaged the covers into sibilance, a susurrus. In that one-night dream I was becoming a word, an inarticulate sound like "ssss" as he poured me into speech. As when children speak through paper cups linked by string I felt like I was at the other end of the line, listening, unable to talk back as I waited with the cup to my ear but maybe, at any moment, about to put it to my mouth and whisper back when the time came for my response. I felt like a rocky abyss of stone raised to echo back, about to reply to his desire with my own. And then, as he shook me and pushed my legs backwards, his hands on my inner thighs and him posturing up on his knees, erect above me, he came. Leaning back and grunting and loudly vocalizing his release, he pushed my legs right back—and in the silence of a photograph I bust a seam. With a faraway agony a little tear, a fingernail across, pursed its lips at the top of my pelvis, just in front of my hip joint, and the occasional glint of metal shone through from inside as I palpated in his wake.

I couldn't believe it. I could see a part of myself that I was never meant to see. And as it glinted there in the dim light I desperately wanted him not to see it, to move myself into action and shake a hand out and pull the blanket over to cover the gash, to hide my shame of breaking for him and revealing something I ought to have kept hidden. Fuck fuck fuck.

He walked off naked to the bathroom, and then came over to tuck us into bed together. It was then he noticed the tear. He looked at it, his hands pausing in the air in pulling the blanket over us, and then he stroked it, first across the top before inserting his finger and feeling the cold metal inside. Then he said "fuck" in a whisper, and looked at me, and turned off the light and held me, and pulled the covers over, and went to sleep.

The next morning he woke up around ten, drank his coffee (it wasn't a coffee day for me, and I was left in the unmade bed), and then I heard him pick up his keys and leave the apartment. He returned about an hour later with two take away coffees and a rustling white grocery bag which he brought into the bedroom and turned out on the bed in front of me.

There was lipstick, make up of various kinds, and a hand mirror. He propped me up opposite him in my spoked wooden chair while he sat down on the bed and picked up the items one by one, looking at each of them carefully. Then he looked at my tear in the daylight, creased closed now as I sat up, and ran his finger across the upraised, sharper burrs of silicone at the edges of the gash.

'FOUNDATION: MAC STUDIO FIX POWDER PLUS FOUNDATION'

J selected a flat, shiny, geometric box and opened it, revealing a mirror inside the lid and some skin-colored dusty-looking pigment on a hinged flap in the middle with a thin, pale white sponge below. He took up the sponge gingerly, between finger and thumb, and waved it, making it flap and flop. Then he rubbed it into the powdered make up and wiped it onto my face; a streak on each cheek, one across my forehead and one under my chin. The sponge felt cool and extremely soft, and once he had made these initial streaks he began, very lightly, almost nothingly at first, to spread them out in widening spirals. This felt great, and made me super sensitive to every curvature and valley in my face, like, the whole landscape of it, in ways that I hadn't been before. My rounded and prominent cheekbones, my smooth forehead, lightly domed, and then the sink towards my eye sockets, my orbital margins feeling gently delineated and rounded out. Of course, I probably didn't have orbital margins, or cheekbones, or anything like that. I didn't know what I had, but I didn't feel this put me back much. J, surely, didn't know for certain what he had, and could never see it himself, right? He could never inspect or look at his face directly, just as I couldn't mine, and while he might at some point get an x-ray or whatever he would never, as I couldn't, be able to three-dimensionally figure his skull first-hand. No one can, because the only skull you can never see is your own. As he applied more foundation my skin started to feel heavy, and a little dirty, and he spread a little of the powder down on my neck, pressing it along the sides of my trachea and what felt like ligaments there.

'BLUSHER L'Oréal Paris le blush 160 TRUE MATCH'

After carefully replacing the foundation he unscrewed a fat brush from a cap, saying "Now for your blusher, my dear." He said it in a funny tone. Then he picked up another flat compartment, a metallic cylinder this time, and opened it, revealing a color— the surface slightly concave—like that of a small, dried, unblown rosebud (one had blown in through the window and onto the sill once while I sat by in my chair). But he began, at first, merely to brush my face without dipping the bristles into the pigment, stroking it gently with a wonderfully soft tickling across each of my cheeks then rustling it vigorously, with an amused expression on his face, across my nose and in my eyes. Nothing had ever really touched my eyes before, and the brush made no noise as the bristles pressed against their glassy surfaces, turning my vision into god's view of a wheat field, so up close. When he did put on the blusher he did it in two dabs, one on each cheekbone, the brush expanding and flattening against my lovely round cheeks with a complex pricking and a pushing, a spreading feeling. Then he dusted me with it, and the brush felt great, frisking my face just where it needed it—not to be scratched, but where it needed to be rustled so gently just like this, the brush creating the itch even as it relieved it.

When he stopped he looked at me, grasping my chin in his hand and turning my face up a little and to the left and right, so he could see it in better light. He looked pleased, but then reached towards my eye with a pincing finger and thumb and pressed his digits into the top of my cheek, scratching me slightly with an unkempt nail, and removed a stray bristle left by the brush. Over the spot he made a single, dainty flick, his wrist a little bent forward and camp, to blend in the red again. I wondered whether he was doing a good job. He seemed to know what he was up to, but wore this kind of vague, dreamy expression with something of the blankness he got while playing the saxophone, but less of the beauty.

'EYELINER L'Oréal Paris COLOR RICHE le smoky'

Next he took up a short black pencil, pulling off its clear plastic top, then started drawing what felt like lines under my eyes. The skin below them pulled and tugged a little, pressed by the hard, almost-sharp nib, and he peered at my face, at its surface but not at me. The nib felt too dry and snagged my skin. It was weird having him look at me, inspect me as though I couldn't see him. And now I was restless, more than I usually was, to see myself. He moved back to look at me, studying. "I paid extra for the veins in your eyes" he said. What did he mean? Licking his lips he leaned in and kissed me hard, passionately, his hand on the back of my head, in my hair. Maybe I looked beautiful.

'MASCARA L'Oréal Paris SUPERLINER Blackbuster'

This instrument was long and thin, and looked like a miniature bottle-brush covered in sticky black gunk. He applied it to my eyelashes, curling the top ones up, the bottom ones down, and getting a bit of this inky crap on my eyeball, that I could feel and just about see like some tar stain on my glossy eyes. It stung, and I got worried that some of it would slip down, real slow, and kind of fill the gap between my eyelid and the bottom of my eyeball and sort of slide in there and drip into the crevice, losing itself somewhere in the ambiguities of my body and staining me inside. My lashes tickled and felt kind of scratched by the brush, which was much coarser and had stiffer bristles than any of the others, and they felt gummy and uncomfortable. I worried, too, that he would pull out one or several of my eyelashes doing this, and whether they could ever be replaced or what happened if I lost them. After he was done I could see them, for the first time, at the top and bottom of my vision, a black mess of window dressing out of focus at the sills of my sight.

'LIPSTICK L'Oréal Paris EVA's PURE RED Collection Exclusive'

He picked up a lipstick tube and applied the hard-soft slanted-off cylinder of waxy dark ruby red to my lips. It was a beautiful shape, the end of that lipstick, before he put it on, and I wondered how they cut it so cleanly or how, if they used a mold or something, they ensured it came away so perfect.

I knew all this stuff was called make up. What a word. You couldn't make it up, ha. It's to invent yourself, to make yourself up like you're writing a story and creating a person with those marks, or to be made up by someone else. And it's a reconciliation, to make up with someone, to come together again, remake something upwards that has been dropped and broken on the floor, to stick it back together with pieces of waxy lipstick and foundation dust and painted gloss and make yourself look pretty, put on a special show and as a treat for someone, and then make up with your lipstick kisses on their cheeks, spreading a bit of your making up onto their lips, a bit of your perfumed dust into bloom on their skin, a bit of mascara from your eyelids to their pillow and then to their face after you make out. On the make. We made it. I was made. Up. Or, like, a makeover. To redo creation, over and over again in time: another chance. A fresh start. Or to cover over and cover up, in space: another face. Or else to finish, to create for the last time: the making is over. As I sat there in the chair and thought on it the words spread out to sharpen or highlight other facets of meaning, their cheekbones glinting and shimmering in the light. To make up your mind— with the sly implication that decisions are cosmetic, or cosmetics are decisive. One's physical makeup—what was mine? And I left off wondering, at last, if I had a make—a brand melted into the sole of my foot that I could not see. After applying the finishing touches to my lips J picked up the little plastic hand mirror and held it up opposite me.

I looked totally different. My face was a different color, the shade of a darkened, old apricot: red flushes on my cheeks, trailing into mottled streaks halfway down my neck. My eyes 'popped', their blue gaining the glimmer of jewels behind thick, stuck-together black eyelashes. There was a black smudge in my left eye near the bottom where my iris met the white. My lips were the worst—the shade looked far too dark, even with the new and different dark of my complexion, and it drained the color from my face. My slightly-open mouth (always slightly open, still; half elegantly waiting for a kiss, half dumbly slack-jawed) revealed a smudge of red across the bottom of both of my two front teeth, where J had clumsily tagged them, and on my lips the wax had partly missed and blurred their shape, and they were thicker and fatter now and made it look like I'd been punched in the face and, like, as though the color, shocked, had spread out beneath the skin. I didn't look like a clown—saying that would be too easy, and not right. I looked as though a person with some weird kind of visual dyslexia had dreamed up a person.

For the first time, I got angry. I got angry with J, for doing this to me so clumsily, for turning what could have been such a treat of attention into a travesty, for ruining me up, for not being able to do with paint and dust and wax what he did with his music. I got angry as though I had been waiting for the anger, as though it turned time backwards and toppled dominos back in my psyche, pissing me off for being put upon on too many times, for not having had a say, ever, for all the hours of patience which came crumbling down as the lipstick felt like it was bleeding from my lips in my bobbing, quavering, circularly-cut reflection in the cheap plastic hand-mirror held by his dumb, feminine, roughened but perfect fingers. Most of all, I hated myself. I was angry beyond reason for having this happen, for letting this happen, for there being no controls to stop this kind of thing from occurring—to stop you being put upon like this by a person made god only because he could move. What I hated was this fate.

J leaned in to kiss me, wearing an odd smirk. He slid his lips across mine lasciviously, slipperily, moving his head a little from side to side, then drew back and guffawed, his lips ridiculous and red, like they'd swollen, and he wiped his mouth with the back of his hand. Then he grabbed my head, his hand on the back of my neck, and, turning his face, pressed my lips into the sharp bristle where the top of his beard met his cheek. He pulled back blinking and smiling, before looking at himself in the hand mirror with a silly grin, and there was a lipstick print on his cheek which he wiped off on his sleeve. He paused.

With a dreamy, sick expression as though losing a certain kind of consciousness of himself, he stood up and looked down at me, sagging and motley, seated in front of him. He stayed like this for a few seconds. And then, roughly, he pushed my shoulder, and I fell backwards with the chair.

He had pushed me carelessly, on a whim but not hard, and as I tipped backward I reached a moment of near-equilibrium halfway through the fall. When you receive a sudden shock time slows, or there is suddenly more of it, and the bottom of your stomach is clenched and tugged earthward by an airy fist. Thus I remember that moment, that moment of almost-fall, where the chair itself actually did slow down, tipping on its back legs but as yet uncertain as to whether to return forwards on that fulcrum and throw me against J's midriff, or to close its collapse backwards and spill me on the floor. And if the chair did eventually fall back, was it always going to? Was there ever a point where it could have not fallen backward, my head knocking against the carpet and strands of hair blown up by the fall sticking to my lips and eyelashes, irritating my eyes? There isn't a tense to express that idea, but there should be. Was it always going *to have fallen* back?

It did. I settled on the floor. And he left. My hair began to gradually spread across my face, occasionally stirring with the wind from the window, or the flap of a door, or simply the current of his passage through the room, for days. My legs had flopped to one side, in very loose fetal, but my arms were spread pretty wide, halfway up and level with my shoulders, as though I was still falling, lifting them out in shock and trying to rebalance myself, or perhaps as though I were poised in an energetic, puppet's shrug, a total resignation to what was happening—what had happened. J came and went, as usual, and stopped, once, a couple of days later, on his passage through the bedroom, to look at me for a few seconds, an unreadably blank expression on his face. But most of the time it was just me and the ceiling. My neck was slightly bent forward against something behind me, my chin almost touching my chest, and so I had a diagonal view across the room looking towards where the ceiling met the opposite wall. Against it was a cheap, metal desk from Ikea with an Apple MacBook computer and three thick box folders for papers in purple, green and blue. There were often mugs and glasses left on the desk, and sometimes tissues too, and it was there that I saw J masturbate for the first time.

It was late at night when he came back and came in and swung his black, metal-seamed saxophone case into the corner next to the desk. He went back out again and I could hear the shower running. A while later it shut off, and after a minute or two he returned with a towel around his waist, his tits wobbling a little, then took it off and dried himself, particularly the splashed droplets on his back, on his shoulder-blades and on his stringy, taut musician's trapezii which were permanently, perhaps, tightened a little from holding his saxophone up all the time. His small penis was wagging out of its thick bushel of hair. Then, naked, he grabbed the box of Kleenex ('man size') from the bedside table and sat down in front of the computer. To start with he clicked often and the screen, from what I could see, was covered with geometrically-arranged rows of small pictures, something like the wall of a closely-covered gallery but regimented, mathematical. Each identically-sized frame— these sample portraits, exact reduction reproductions—showed a piece of the video you could watch there if you clicked on it, and they seemed to slip and change when J moved the little white arrow over them, like a Cubist painting, split up and staggered. Here was sex in the abstract, its acts and movements tugged out of themselves and their meaningful individual situations into a blur of parts and taxonomical settings.

Clicking, he sat there. Gradually, as he clicked, he hunched over more and more until he looked from behind like a hunchback or homunculus, his other elbow splayed and moving as he rubbed and tugged on himself sporadically. Then a video came to fill the whole screen, twitchy and schizophrenic at first as J clicked through it, pausing barely long enough with each click for me to see what was going on but able himself, it seemed, to judge each moment almost instantaneously by a hyped, hyper-focused rationale of his own. The audio lagged a little behind his clicks—not out of sync but taking a while to load or whatever, and sometimes only doing so when he'd skipped forwards again, so there'd be the sound of a cock choking a throat—suddenly abrupted—over a kiss.

J found a spot to settle on, and began to watch a man having sex with a woman. She was on a beige couch in some large, white room with high ceilings and internal stairs of metal and glass in the background, and she started bent over, wearing only black high heels, her very straight blonde hair with dark roots swishing and shaking inaudibly below the other noises they were making, the creaking and slapping, her weird, abstracted and idealized cries, a repetitive "yuh" that changed to a deep primal groaning that had something of a farmyard moo. Seeing the woman move, naked, seeing all of this for the first time, was a revelation to me. It better explained what I was—something, probably, that could never move like this, how the woman in the movie did, just something that would be forever how I already was. J wasn't teaching me anything through sex, after all. He was doing just what he was doing now.

The woman on the film was, you see, particularly organic. The male in the picture was vast, his hamstrings popping out like pulleys, his buttocks bunching and inflating like bellows, the straps of his deltoids—much more aggressive and defined than J's—tightening and loosening with nictitative frequency. His musculature made him look like a machine with the mechanism exposed for show, like a watch with a glass back or a motorbike with a cutaway engine. Compared to him she was like a yogurt, some smooth, ultra-organic thing of curves and hypertrophic globular bloomings. As he had sex with her he mumbled incessantly, unintelligibly to himself, as J sometimes did during sex, and you could catch the occasional phrase—"like it" "fuck you" "your tight pussy"—but all the rest was burnt off, like the exhaust, the steam of his billowing motor. These noises were just the waste, the sound and fumes and hum of an engine, incidental to its function but goading it on, a separate cogwheel turning locked to the first but aimlessly in air, squeaking to nothing and no one and distracted from itself.

I said she was organic. She looked like that mainly because she'd become attached to his power, to the wheels and pistons of his working and become caught up in them, stuck onto him as part of his puzzle of machinery. Temporarily absorbed into his mechanics she was the missing piece, and I felt he would otherwise just have been blasting away at air perpetually, inexorably, before she arrived. She just kind of filled a hole in the film.

But, weirdly, it was her lifelikeness that made her look somehow fake in this composition, a ballet dancer fumbling two steps behind the rest who was rushed into each position as he changed his mode and his switches flicked, suddenly thrusting her into a new pose that she had to hustle to get right lest his proboscis thrust her innards at an unpropitious angle. It was clear that she could be bruised in this exchange, but only blushingly red and superficially, with plasticated hemorrhage that would never, somehow, register the complexity of events and only unsatisfactorily expose the photographic encounter for later in cloudy nebulae on her skin—for later when, sipping tea at home and shifting every few minutes on the gray and prickly cotton of her couch, her eyes would glaze in rapt, almost ecstatic, boredom, boredom that glancingly swathed the girl from the mechanics of it all.

And then, as the intensity increased like someone was turning a knob, she was the machine he was operating and he was a cog hotwiring her. Breaking through her stereo again and again and busting the plastic panels and pulling out the wires and tangling them and mashing them frisky like snakes in his fists, a horny Hercules tearing them together and cleaving into automotive pneumatics, pumping and drilling at the pistons and revving them until they were overclocked and gasping spluttering gasoline and almost catching fire with the blazing heat. Then crunching the gas and clutch and brakes into the floor all at once and charging like a bull with her down through the road and asphalt, tires grating the gutter and peeling the hubcaps from the wheels like crushed eggshells smattered by the wind, masticating the entire vehicle into vehicular propulsion, gassing into the works and ejaculating inside the open, hydraulic, endlessly fluid engine as parts of her she had never heard about or understood evaporated in the smog. She became his contraption and understood the purpose he raped upon her as the purpose she had been meant to have—a false inference. Through the fence and into the ditch. He was a special effect waiting to happen and she was the detonator.

As she exploded into screams on the screen and the man pulled out, thrusting her to her knees by her hair bunched tight in his fist to impregnate her face and to paint, to slur, slew and slaw himself willy-nilly across her face and cheeks, J sprang upwards into a crouch, his own stringy hamstrings sticking out amongst the hair on his legs matted sweaty from sitting down, pushing up hunched as though restricted by invisible elastic, and he grunted himself out, very quietly, into a messy fistful flower of Kleenex, 'man size'.

He balled up the tissues and dropped them on the table, leaving the moldy chlorine smell to gradually fill the room with its musk throughout the night. He closed the laptop, that window onto another place, an impossible vista that made it hard to think those events just seen had actually happened somewhere, and got into bed, wrapping the covers over his head, and went to sleep.

I lay on the floor where I had fallen for days more, a thin film of dust gathering on my eyes. The make up started to gradually feel caked and dry, tightening the skin together not locally but all over, all at once, the lipstick on my lips a hardening, itchy coating that starched the corners of my mouth. I was dry anyway, of course, but there was something aggressive about this dryness. A window pane isn't as dry as the sand it's made from, there's something that at least feels like liquid wetness about its surface, whereas sand, or salt, or arid spices, all seem somehow much dryer than that. That was how my face felt dry.

I stared at where the wall met the ceiling opposite me above the desk, seeing him come and go across my vision, rarely in the center where I could see him properly but badly framed; his face just at the edges of my sight or turned unknowably away. Looking at the join of ceiling and wall I thought of all the other apartments in the building, below and above this one—which I assumed had to be there—and of rooms in other houses and other buildings of almost inconceivable variety and character—infinite, not because there were an infinite number of houses but because of the numberless detail, the numberless levels of interest and magnification and history to focus upon in every item or splinter or brick or grain of plaster dust. I wondered whether there were any other dolls out there—whether, even, somewhere in the world there was another doll imagining the same thing. I wondered whether she imagined me imagining her imagining me imagining her, whether this reflective layer had occurred to her imagination, and whether it had occurred to her that it might also have occurred to me. I was wondering whether she had come to see that these layers upon layers of possible thoughts and connections could be limitless, and that really the important thing was to realize that the other person might have realized this apprehension of limitlessness too, so instead of having to talk through everything if you met you might simply greet them with a wordless expression that told of your joint knowledge.

I told you that while I dreamed, I'm not sure I ever slept. That is true; I was always awake and responsive to stimuli, ready to react or be roused by J kissing me or fucking me, cuddling me or, later, brushing past me as I lay on the floor. But when I say I dreamed, I can't, you know, be totally sure. Dreams were one of the few things I hadn't amassed enough experience of to conceive completely—obviously I couldn't talk with other people about theirs, or tell them mine, and while I'd seen bits on TV that seemed to be dream sequences, nothing in my mind ever had their crystalline, HD perfection, or, as they were sometimes also portrayed, their blurred, underwater confusion of sight and sound. What I did have were prolonged ruminations, dreamlike to the extent that I lost a certain amount of attention to my senses; I forgot where I was placed and what I was looking at until I emerged from the reverie, and although in emerging it wasn't exactly as though a light was coming on—onto whatever I was looking at, since it had always, in a way, been there in front of me—that wouldn't nevertheless be a totally stupid way to put it. The shock of return was like turning—or being turned—knowing that something you're very familiar with is just there, only to find it gone; the furniture has been rearranged or the bus stop demolished. That surprise of meeting a reality obstinate to your fancy.

In one of these subtle reveries, one which I could never reconjure afterwards in its full monochrome brilliance and sparkling light, I dreamed that I was running on the ice with J. I dreamed about running naked on the ice with him, illuminated by a floodlight that moved but is not a spotlight, a perfect kind of halogen dream light, and they're running naked on the ice and neither of us can really feel the cold, in that they can feel it and

69

it doesn't hurt them—both our weirdly stupid, asymmetrically stupid bodies running, kind of sliding, a kind of motion left dream-ambiguous, on the ice together, the blank snow-topped fingers of wintry trees illuminated then banished flashing in the floodlight behind them, and they're both in the third-person, and she can see herself and her joints supporting herself and her eyes smiling as she skates barefoot across the ice. That was her reverie.

I began to drift out to the edges of his life. After days on the floor he moved me and I was left hanging off the bed, my limbs trailing on the carpet like willow branches weeping into the river before they break off and are swept away. A splish-splash-drip-drop—I was washed into the shallows, the lees lapping at the leas in the last lease of autumn, whirling me in eddies past, over, under and among clothes, ligatures, pages, debris, flowers and buds shaken from the hats of boaters oblivious. I drifted on his stern sheets, overtopped cascades of cloth, crashed down into the carpet, flooded to the floor. My hand, a dumb mute oar, lay open to receive the spar of the bedpost but the river came into spate in spite of me. I found the delta of the hall, and then I slipped out to sea.

I was waved back by the door as I leaned against it and he pulled it open with me, then ran me aground in closing. His will was like the sea, mutable and immutable, a tide of desire that had drawn me in, the pebbles' sibilance shushing whatever protests I might have made with one long suck and I had to float. Against the cliff of the bed's bottom boards I was sucked and sucked again. Tides turned and ripped, they skirted and scudded the skirting boards. His kisses dried on me like barnacles, periwinkles, patches of dark lichen appearing as crusts on rocks. I drifted as a piece of flotsam, jetsam, ligan, derelict; first crumpled like a used tissue, foot touching face, then sinking face down and ass up, nosing the seabed. My hair a crow's nest, my ribcage an empty hull, the beams and bulwarks sharpened into splinters by the sea, and the breastbone at my bow come to rest half-buried in a bank in the great beneath. Dust covered my eyes, sand clogged my portholes, and soon I was left blind with silt.

At these depths the aquatic life experiences no light other than bioluminescence. After days and nights in darkness I was picked up, stirred from the ocean floor. Dredged by an errant wave, the result of some plate's sudden crack, or just a whim of water beaten back. Floating, in a progression of ebbing and flowing, I was washed, further and further ashore until the foam stroked my ankles in parting. I had just a mouth full of sandy dust, aground at last, my legs behind my head. Washed up inside a closet and beached upon its continental shelf.

Marooned and castaway, there I became most dry. Desiccant and parched, rinsed in the spume at this high water mark on a shelf behind the open door of the cliff's cave, as it was shut and opened and shut again by the sea closing its great mouth—I languished. Washed finally ashore, shored up, unsure and then certain that I was stopped. I could not breathe, I cannot drown or sink, I can only corrode in his salty water like a coconut husk or some straw dame de voyage, a thing rutted and sparred like a strut from a broken vessel. I will sleep across the shelves of sunken seas.

Love permits no conclusions.

II

You are interested in the Speaking Clock. You remember your grandfather first telling you about it as you sat on his knee, with your brown curls, which were looser then, falling around your face. At least, that's how you remember it, but who truly remembers brown curls falling around their face, and sitting on their grandfather's knee?

You do remember your grandfather's drawing room. Grammy had fallen and had a heart attack, or had a heart attack and fallen, and been killed twice over; you remember grandpa being proud of it as a testament to her hardiness. So you don't recall much of Grammy. Just a ragged, dreamy silhouette in a chair, the angle at which she was sunken back into it, that unusual slouch—the one first affected in slatternly youth and then affecting in its old age echo—and something in her proportions, colouring or dress that reminds you now of pictures of Queen Victoria. But grandpa you do remember. His big cheeks were made bigger by his round white beard which grew, with thick hairs, more outwards than downwards. White hairs trumpeted too out of his nose, and his white eyebrows which curled upwards at the end were a Chinese dragon's and still had streaks of black in them until the day he died. He was proud of those as well. He was a proud man.

Every surface in the drawing room seemed covered in thread. The frayed white doily on the coffee table; the faded patchwork cover of the sofa; the copious cushions; the tea cosies—relics, all, of Grammy's knitting, (all those knots she had fastened to tie herself into the world)—and then grandpa's worn kippah with the lonesome, touching black threads that curled off it at the edges. Because of all this stuff, and the walls of 'Classics' bound in red cloth (though it was well known that grandpa only read *Don Quixote* over and over), the room had a dull, warm acoustic. Voices were so lost in the tangle of threads that the space sounded infinite. Sound was absorbed so well that, if you closed your eyes, it seemed as if there were no walls at all and that the room just went on for ever and ever. That warm closeness, the feel of the threads, the smell of mint tea and pot-pourri and the sound effect of immaculate distance created a sense-experience unlike any other, a kind of nowhere in a little room. These particular qualities of sensation were accompanied by a sense of your own limitlessness which you lost as you got older, of avenues of exciting possibility through which you would yet be kept safe. But back then you felt innocent and not self-regarding; there were no echoes of self-consciousness offering shame or critique when you were a child in your grandfather's drawing room. Those only came later.

As you sat on your grandfather's knee, on his thick brown corduroy trousers, beneath which the shiny, hairless shins that were somewhat reflective, worn smooth by seventy years in the service of a man who, from manhood, wore his black socks pulled all the way up—as you sat there (yes you; very you; very now), he would tell you about his life. In particular, you remember, he would tell you of the Speaking Clock. It sounded then like a piece of magic, the way he told of it. It isn't so far off magic now. As an ideal, at least.

For almost thirty years your grandfather was 'Technical Engineer' on the Speaking Clock, starting at some point, you'd have to guess, in the early fifties. There is a photograph that he used to show you in which he's wearing a jaunty, floppy flat cap (underneath which, he boasted, his kippah) and standing in front of the machine. This photo used to sit on the side table next to your grandfather's chair in his drawing room. You believe your father has it now. In the picture your grandfather is a young man with wavy, possibly oiled, jet black hair and is wearing overalls. His face has an odd expression and he is striking an odd attitude, one hand leaning on the edge of the table holding the machine, the other by his hip, palm curled away and back as though cupping something. His expression is at odds with his pose, for his body is attempting a relaxed, swaggering stance of casual mastery and elegance—albeit rather stiffly—yet his eyes look startled. They are still the eyes of a Jewish boy whose family fled to London and who was then sent off with a trainload of British goy children to a school near Fort William—a school which was more like a boarding house with a library. Perhaps that's where he discovered *Don Quixote* for the first time, as a comfort. You never asked.

The machine behind him in the photograph, the first Speaking Clock, is laid out on a table, and resembles something from the set of an early sci-fi film. It is a mechanism of motors, glass discs, photocells, valves and wheels that told the time accurate to one-tenth of a second. There was something it reminded you of as a child, or which you'd always associated with the way it looked in the photograph but never put your finger on until later—indeed, it is definitely possible that you invented the connection only in retrospect, it's hard to tell. In your imagination it is tied up with a loom. The rods and axles; the spinning discs and the cogs; the way it was laid out on the table top at the chest height of a seated person; it looked like a loom for sound, stitching it together with its wheels. In fact, not for sound merely—it looked as though it was a loom for time; not monitoring it, not just counting it, but making it. Making it up and putting it together. When you first heard the adage 'a stitch in time', with the misunderstanding that a child's imagination can bring, you thought it meant a stitch sewn into time, as if time was a fabric, and not 'before it's too late'.

And, indeed, the Speaking Clock did stitch—stitched a voice together. The first voice of the Speaking Clock, your grandfather said, was that of a woman called Ethel Jane Cain—with that strange Torah surname—who won the job through a competition in 1936. She received ten guineas for her trouble. The Speaking Clock, your grandfather would tell you, had four discs. Two were used for the minutes, one for the hours, one for the seconds. The announcements would go "At the third stroke it will be twelve, thirty-five, and thirty seconds precisely... beep... beep... beeeep." They would stitch together a sentence on your grandfather's loom.

You never heard it when grandpa was alive but you called it one afternoon this January. One afternoon, apropos of nothing, the desire came to you; a specific, fully-formed action arising from a general urge. It occurred to you to call your family but you didn't want to, needing instead to commune with yourself: to be alone in company or, rather, in company alone. There are other ways of doing this—listening to music, reading a book, or playing the saxophone—but this is the one that came to you, with an attractively mournful quality about it, as if your grandfather would be watching you making the call.

You have to look up on the internet how to dial it—clearly you aren't doing this to find out the time—and you know it won't be the same voice your grandfather heard when he was working on it. That woman is dead. You don't know whether her voice outlasted her at all. You do know that it's a new lady now. You called her up. There's is an interesting turn of phrase. You summoned her. You called her up.

But there was no 'her' there. You listen for a voice that has the ghost of human giving in it, and a voice that wouldn't listen back. You had still wanted her to be yours, to serve you only, and when you listen she comes on mid-sentence, as she goes on telling the time to others and to no one when no one calls. You listen to each number she reads, hoping that the absence of emotion in the "thirty" will be replaced by a glimmer of something in the "forty"; listen for the flicker of sarcasm or knowing irony; a lip peeling open at the corner like a steamed envelope, revealing a smile; a smile the space of which you could hear—which you could see, hearingly. You hope that the dull chime of the singular "one" might find a more welcoming echo in the "two", its disciple and opposite; the beginning of something hopeful, a warmth gathering with time. You listen in for a voice giving the word "stroke" the slightest caress of a faintly rolled R, to hear the rough drag of a tongue on the roof of a delicate female mouth. You strain to find some relish in the three sharp syllables of "precisely", their exactitude and the lick into the warm vowel of "-ly" shutting off the hissing static of the two Ss—to hear some human relish of the precision of the pronunciation itself. But it was as cold as ice. You heard nothing. No space. No time. No person there actually saying things in a room with her own thoughts and feelings, primly dressed for the job after winning the competition and before leaving the offices to which she'd been summoned, after merely a few hours of recording. And then her feeling of slight disappointment, having taken the rest of the day off work and now with nobody to spend it with and nothing to do but to look in the windows of flower shops, at the pre-written wishes on the cards, and to wonder whether, after all, she truly did want to be heard by millions, and thinking that if she died she would still, still be heard. You want to hear something of this in the voice, but you do not.

The magical notion you had received from your grandfather— the idea almost of automatic sentience through recorded voice, when recorded sound still felt like a miracle—that ideal felt sullied and guilty, like rereading a book when you are older that you had lived inside as a child and feeling that there must be some mistake, that you must have an abridged version, that the world you had known was not responsible to these meagre scratchings on the page. There was something about the voice that wasn't merely non-human but inhuman. The tiny differences in timing from natural speech due to the way the sentences were knitted together were so miniscule you couldn't have stated them clearly or put your finger on the exact moments of fracture, on the precise faults in cadence, but they were felt in your stomach as something just fundamentally awry, as a dog can know something is wrong but doesn't know what it is or how he knows it. It made the voice horrible, uncanny. Like human, so like but without being that it was a grotesque, monstrous parody. And you felt the fear that copying can inspire—like a schoolmate aping every change in your face until your expressions are no longer your own.

A few days afterwards you ordered a sex doll. You didn't note any resemblance between the two actions. In fact, one thing that the two acts shared was the lack of examination you expended on the intentions behind each of them. Ordering a doll was akin to making your bed, tidying your apartment, or putting on your favourite boxer shorts before a night out; it was done with a sense of unspecified anticipation that you might not even acknowledge to yourself, or the implications of which you don't look at too closely. With the boxer shorts it's because you're hoping to get lucky. With ordering a doll it was something like that too.

By the time you enter the website you have already exchanged yourself for something thin, white, flat and directional. In this place you are a white arrowhead, brought to a sharpened, pixellated point. You are a figure that only exists in relation to other things as targets; a shape that gestures away from itself; the very picture of desire. It is the unique nature of signs which point that they act to efface themselves. There. When you hover over the button that says ENTER REALDOLL you take the first step to embodiment and figuration; the cursor turns from an arrowhead to a hand with a pointing finger. Hours spent on the internet—days, rather, if not months—have developed in you a honed mental apprehension for where there is a button or a link on a page, an ability to feel the surface of a site for invisible indentations that is almost another sense, to run fine fingers down the subtly embossed surface. Your representative in this world is yet mute, wordless—children learn to point before they learn to speak—but has changed to this hand to suggest the tactile ridges of a button inside the flat screen. A flick to the gesture of a single-finger caress; a tap on the shoulder for a discreet word; a finger raised in discussion to prefigure a subtle point of information. You caress the button with your cursor. The word itself soothes with its seductive inconsequence: the movements of a cursor must be by nature cursory. In a browser you can only be browsing. The language flatters your intentions with a cool insouciance; an impartiality of passion; you could take it or leave it. With a satisfying click of your real finger on your real mouse giving sound to the silent click of the panel, you depress the sign. ENTER REALDOLL.

The interior has elegant black cherry wood panelling as background, eternally darkening to the upper, unattainable reaches above the top of the page. The grain of the wood is complexly rendered, but careful inspection of its patterns reveals that the boards repeat themselves further down, then repeat themselves again on the longer pages—like identical snowflakes or déjà vu— the same cat passing you twice. The header announces "realdoll", and a panel below changes every few seconds, presenting a loop of different models. AIMEE. STEPHANIE. *Club* realdoll. realdoll Affiliate Program. TANYA.

Deliberately you do not go for the dolls first, titillating yourself by drawing out the pleasure of purchase. You head instead for the ancillary products, enjoying the possibility of their possession—knowing you have this money freely to spend—even though you will not buy any of them. But for now everything here is yours in potentiality, and with that knowledge you can sample the satisfaction of ownership. Reviewing the entire site in a logical order also satisfies your completism, offering the further pleasure of methodical procedure, inevitably chastened by the anxious stress of compulsion. You shall start with those pages in which you have only a cursory, curious interest before homing in on your prize;

then you will proceed to the more careful, irrevocable choices until you drop a body in your little shopping cart. The sensation of desire restrained by meticulous order is both enervating and arousing simultaneously, like a strip-tease's slow undoing of frustration, just as it arouses desire in inverted contrapunto to a climax. On offer we have TORSOS – DOLL ACCESSORIES – EXTRA FACES – SEX TOYS – TRANSGENDER/ CD. You select TORSOS.

The first item is BOTTOMS-UP "MALE", and the photograph is a picture of a hairless white male torso with its buttocks and arsehole open to the camera, ample, stringy testicles hanging below like dropping fruit. Repugnant. You make a face and scroll all the way down to the bottom of the page, although it's not clear what you must hurry to escape. The last item is not, in fact, a torso, but PAIR OF FEET, $299. "These beautiful feet are available in either size 7 or 8 with your choice of skin tone and nail polish color. Shoes are not included." Only a right foot is shown in the picture, from different angles, and wearing a transparent, plasticky high-heel with the word "SEX" running down the stiletto. The feet are cut off just above the ankle, flawless skin continuing over the severed cross-section as if the foot were a complete organism, or a photograph made real; an appendage from a picture-world where things really do cut off seamlessly at the edges of the frame.

The torsos are severed in the same manner. The FEMALE DELUXE REALDOLL TORSO ($2,999 with head, $2,499 without) is available in two body types: athletic or voluptuous. You don't know why anyone would choose athletic. What limbs the torsos have end at the shoulders and at the tops of the thighs, but here the same style of dismemberment as the foot voids the illusion of integrity in a way that makes it hard for you to comprehend any desire for such a torso. It is one thing for a foot (and you will never understand those guys anyway), but here is a near-complete doll with falsity so vividly on view, a smooth face of skin where there should be splintered bone and gushing blood or scar tissue were she really severed. The effect so pointlessly obliterates the mystery of the interior, and to you it is uncanny, like meeting someone without a bellybutton but just a smooth, continuous wall. Not that these creatures need bellybuttons though, either. Like Adam and Eve. But why would you not spend the extra money and purchase limbs? Seeing it flipped over, however, you realise that this design does have some purpose: a further photograph shows one of the torsos laid face-down on a tabletop, ass-up towards the camera, with a head, this time, of which only a mass of shiny wig hair is visible. The thigh cross-sections meet the table exactly and the tits support the upper part of the torso, like a piece of furniture with four legs. You find yourself shocked, to your own surprise, that it should be made with such design convenience in mind and meet the table so exactly.

All these parts have their price. Behind the scenes equations of lust must run. The relative desirability of a foot to a torso, an extra piercing to a larger cup size, counted up against how difficult and expensive each piece is to produce. Payment is already abstraction—those beautiful licks and your breath played through the saxophone was the first thing reduced to single, summable value. It is an infinite, almost holy activity given a figure on a fungible plane. A figure that is the opposite of what that word suggests. Here you are to restore the numbers to embodiment— after the first shift from arrow to mute hand, now your value is to become numerical, and the words are provided to articulate your desire. You will turn those figures to a figure again.

In choosing your doll, at last, it is reassuring to find that, where your lust had been amorphous, here it is given words and shape. Part of the service is in the furnishment of a vocabulary to your desire, the provision of its form. Your ideal of facial beauty is, it turns out, Stacy—Face P. The ideal figure, Body D (with buttocks gels). Your skin tone; fair; your lip colour, natural. The vaginal inserts bring what you would never even have tried to articulate to yourself into the bright light of language. They are removable vaginas, and plucked from their cavities they resemble thick-stemmed poppies, tubes with burgeoning fleshy flowerheads looking as if made to blow and scatter rather than to engulf. You had not even given thought to what you liked in a pussy, but you come to find it out now even as you select it, and after a brief struggle between vaginal inserts B and G you decide that the clit is too small and secret on the former. It brings satisfaction and strange relief to know that the pussy style you most like in a woman is insert G, to have these craftsman anatomise a previously deep and shifting desire.

At the end of filling in the digital form with these specifications you feel that you have been in the hands of a master tailor, a man of deference cutting a suit to fit you, offering options at your grace and leisure, some of which you accept, others that you discerningly decline. Would you like stylised custom make up with her, sir? No, thank you. Hi-Realism Eyes for an additional fifty dollars? Yes, Sky Blue please, and with the veins upgrade option—I'll pay the extra $25. Very well sir—a cup size larger for $800.00? Certainly not. Very good sir. And shaved as standard or pubic hair? Pubic hair, certainly; blonde, trimmed. Excellent taste sir, if I may say so. We are so rarely graced with such a tasteful and exacting palate.

Here, you realise in a moment of exquisite insight, desire has been tamed—not twisted. It is no longer an intuitive, incontinent response of feeling—'*she* is a woman I want'—but an implemented act, the zeugma of specification to desire—'I want her *to be like this*':

Female FaceX RD2	Stacy – Face P (RD2 Magnet Style Face)
Female Body RD2	Body D (with buttocks gels)
Skin Tone	Fair
Lip Color	Natural
Fingernail/Toenail Color	Natural
RD2 Eye Color	Blue
Hi-Realism Eyes (additional $50.00)	Sky Blue (+$50.00)
Eye Upgrades/Options (ONLY AVAILABLE FOR HI REALISM EYES)	Veins upgrade option (+$25.00)
Hand Painted Acrylic Eyes	None
Fixed Eyes	No fixed eyes option (default)
Hand Punched Eyebrows	None
Stylized Custom Makeup	None
Hair Options	Standard Options – Please Select Style/Color Below
Hair Color	Light Blonde
Hair Style	Style 0718
Vaginal Insert Style (RD2)	Insert Type "G"
Additional RD2 Inserts	None (default)
Duracast for Hands/Feet	Both (Hands & Feet)

OPTIONAL EXTRAS FOR YOUR DOLL (optional extras)

Elf Ears	No elf ears
ID Lube	None

Custom Freckles	No Custom Freckles
1 Cup Size Larger Breasts	Standard Breast Size
Custom Nipples	Super Puffy L (+$99.00)
Custom Nipple Color	Cerulean Pink(+$25.00)
Female Pubic Hair Option	Blonde Trimmed (+$100.00)
RealDoll2 Optional	
Transgender Converter	No Transgender Converter (default)
Include Doll Stand	No Stand (default)
Club RealDoll VIP Access	No Subscription
RealDoll Express Option++	No Express Option (default)

Sub Total (Excl. TAX (tax charged for California residents only))	$6798.00
Shipping & Handling	$550.00
Total	$7348.00

And then, once ordered, and despite its enormous expense, you forgot about it. It simply left your mind. But the world had not forgotten about your order. Ores are pulled bodily out of the ground, disinterred and resurrected then melted, smelted and refined. Money changes hands; wheels and tyres commit a million revolutions; thousands of treads at regulation depth run over the roads and kick up gravel and scree. Metals find their moulds and are lathed; stainless steel is poured in accordance with equations once drawn in chalk on blackboards to make it light and strong, a skeleton with a mirrored surface. That reflection is hidden in flesh, rubber heated, injected hot and crammed into the cavities of a full iron maiden brimming with liquid tissue, slick inside with petroleum; opening, it flops out bald and must be peeled off the walls. Extracted, it is rinsed free of lubricant. The skin tags, each small flag and variation, each beauty spot, each accident of form in bur or offcut—all are pared by the craftsman's knife and dropped into a bucket full of mingled, discarded flesh. Hung from chains as at the abattoir, it swings and sways suspended in the air before you, swaying in and out of shadows; changing light animates its face and flashes in its eyes, which are beginning to stare wide with no sill of lashes yet to soften or narrow that gaze. Then the skull is drilled with hair, hair that was shaven so close to the scalp that the electric razor burnt the real women who had sold it; pubic hair the same. And you're giving all those women who gave their heads of hair something too. This is power. This, patronage. Look at what your unconscious has been doing.

While this time passes you're waiting for your head to clear. Only too often, since Margaret perhaps, perhaps before, you've been experiencing these periods of no clarity, no time, no memories. You can't recall what you did yesterday, or the effort is unbearable; your mind turns away, too tired even to shrug shoulders at the effort. Tinnitus begins, and dreams so mundane and close to real life that you confuse the two. You give yourself errands—another coffee, post an invoice, buy bread—going out as many times as possible in the day to help it to pass, to get it done with, to slip out from under the weight and pressure of another set of hours; numbered; countless. You sleep and sleep and then, no matter how much you sleep, you sleepwalk through the days, unable to think clearly, unable to feel deeply, unable to be dynamic on the saxophone, making jokes with friends that fall from your lips without your notice, and you forget how long it's been that you've been this way. It seems no time at all, but you are made to register it by needing, all of a sudden, to cut your nails again, or when you run out of clean socks. The bowl of milk from the muesli you thought you had eaten only yesterday has fermented, moulded and then dried, cracked apart in the bottom of the bowl to form a dirt plain. A fissured terracotta basin, clay wastes, fossilised nuts. Milk going off, turning solid and useless, the use-by dates of things in the fridge changing, jumping in the course of a single afternoon to three weeks ago, the kitchen bin full up so the lid won't close, no more loo paper and you have to use paper towel from the kitchen, your medication running out, the dates on bills you haven't paid. These are the only signs that anything is happening at all.

And then one morning, after weeks of this, you wake up clear. No explanation is offered for it coming on or going off. It just does. Each time it's like this; each time you remember that this is what you have to wait for. It's reasonless, circling. And this morning, the morning you wake up clear, your order is due for delivery today.

What you remember best about her arrival is the way her eyes looked. But it's a memory you've gone over so often it's hard to tell how much of it is real, and how much is a tune you only think you remember when in fact you've been writing it yourself. When she finally comes she slips into your life as though she has always been there. It is hard to imagine a time before her, as it is sometimes with a girlfriend, the way they become a part of you.

Until seeing her the rest of that day is diffracted in the memory. It has, in the calendar of your imagination, the ascendancy of a day off school, spent at home because sick. The sense of reprieve, of a treat, of a skip in the record—and of the sudden dilation of unstructured time, the blurring of memory without the armature of structure. A day both much longer than a school day, because the time in bed was endless in comparison to the length of any lesson, but shorter as well, because there's only one activity marked on the page: lying there, in the stern white sheets, drifting.

Thus the memory of the day of her entrance; a day that was all one swathe. You think that there were two large men who brought the crate—a crate made of a light yellow, splintery wood like pine—up the stairs to your apartment but it's hard to be certain because of how nervous you were. Somehow it came to stand there, ominous, in the middle of the sitting room floor. You do remember that you put on 'Beggars Banquet' by the Stones; to calm or cover the anxiety. And also because you knew she'd hear it; this was how you had wanted to begin. Walking over to your vinyl collection you'd picked the record almost at random—almost. The LP in a white jacket, blank but for the curlicued text of the title and the "R.S.V.P." at the bottom in the style of a formal invitation. You drew the album from its place on the shelf; slid the vinyl from its sleeve; whisked the record out of its paper covering; placed it on the turntable; and then the automatic arm onto it, with the quietest of thuds. You don't remember when you stopped it. The first track was *Sympathy for the Devil*. This was how you wanted to begin.

First there was the rush of Styrofoam as you pried off the front of the crate. The unexpected movement and the sound rushing from inside gave you rather a shock, as though a living object were erupting from within. And then there was the first sight of her, inside a clear plastic bag, latched to the back of the crate by the neck. With the slight shimmer of space and shape created by the lens of the sac the effect was of seeing her from a great distance, optically distorted by miles of thick air. Yet the thing you remember most about those seconds is the way she looked at you—looks at you—when you bend down to peer at her through the plastic, and the way she continues to look at you as you tear through it. It is almost surprising that in tearing the bag you don't tear her into pieces.

You kneel on the floor to look into her face and are met by her gaze and the way her eyes aren't afraid of meeting yours—but do so with diffidence; the way she looks at you is different. People seem so afraid of prolonged eye contact but you crave it and the closeness it implies with a partner. You have often felt as though you'd never had anyone look at you and not pretend that it was a kind of accident, that into yours was just where their eyes fell and that nothing was meant by it. Margaret had been the same. Those women, the other women who had looked at you, had been leery of looking into, rather than just at, your eyes. But now these eyes meet yours and do not turn away. Her gaze is unfocussed, not staring into you deeply and almost unbearably the way a human gaze stares into you but with a more gentle aspect, as though she can see you and is looking at you but, at the same time, is shyly, generously taking her eyes a micron away from yours, coyly and with respect to your dominance—a woman fearful to give away how much she likes you by looking you straight in the face, and yet braving herself to do so all the same.

The next thing you note is her skin. It's perfect, unblemished, such that it loses something of the perspective that the moles, rolls and slack and lines of our thin, storied layer give to a human exterior, and instead her shape floats ambiguously in the box. The Styrofoam is more flawed and burred in its shapes, more roughened than she is. Her hair falls slightly across her face and the ends of it are oddly straight and blunt like hair on a human being when you cut it; not broken, because the ends aren't frayed but pale gold and pristine, but just very straight and falling down under its own light weight, without the grease or curl of living hair which bunches it into locks and strands. It seems more evenly distributed from the head in a way that is hard to put your finger on; neither thicker nor thinner in volume than a head of human hair—they've got that right—but just less organically organised. It is human hair, of course. That's the thing. As it is at her pubis.

You sit back on the sofa opposite her and examine your prize. The excitement of purchase, a dopaminergic thrum of acquisition, has been humming through you, coming now to its height. Stunned by it somewhat, experiencing the kind of euphoria which banishes inhibition, you look at her, and allow her, and what you have done, to wash over you, to appear to you in its real form for the first time. She is there in the box and you are here on the sofa. And as you contemplate these facts you discover that she is a thing apart from you, quite separate, with her own attributes and characteristics. You look at the health of her face, the wide amused curiosity of her eyes—the expression comes close to looking stupid but ultimately doesn't—and the plump, global roundness of her tits. Then it comes to you: she is, of course, American.

You go to the bathroom to start a bath running, light a candle on the cistern, and then turn off the light, which seems to make the sound of the running water louder, the water and the candlelight lapping the walls together. Then you go back to the sitting room to pull her out of her box, spilling Styrofoam. She's blissfully light, and you take her through, and check the temperature with one hand whilst clinging her to your chest with the other, feeling strong and showing your strength to her. Her flesh is creamy, but slightly more frictive than a real woman's, more resistant to touch;

perhaps from the thin, just-noticeable sheen of zinc oxide on her skin that makes it stick a bit. It's there to keep her sterile and it's why you have to wash her. You lower her into the bath and she seems more naked when covered by the warm water in the dark, more potent with heat and mystery. You bathe her a little. And then you try to wash the smell of cigarettes from the fore and middle fingers of your right hand. Planning ahead.

You bend down and press your cheek against hers, feeling it wet against yours, and you hide your face from her in her hair. What now? In imagining her entrance into your life you had come this far and no further. You know only how this first half of the piece you've been playing goes and where it has to end up; it is a record the beginning and ending of which play, but that skips and fritters passages in the middle. You must find what will take you where you want to go; a melody that will fit. You stare at the grid of alabaster tiles on the bathroom wall, flickering in the candlelight into ideal form. The texture and marble speckling of the squares is lost to the dark and the lines abstracted into perfect geometry as the shadows justify any deviance from exact rectitude. She swells there in the bath, not buoyed but for her tits, which are bobbing, and you lose your hand in the water.

After a minute or two of kneeling there, your eyes glazed out of thought on the wall, the passage you have to play comes to you. Leaving her round in the water, deliberately getting up without any explanation and enjoying the mystery you must thus engender as to where you are going, savouring the slight fear she could have of abandonment, you trot out, nimble with inspiration and feeling urgent about it as though she's a waiting guest. You go to the little bookshelf and get out Ovid, sit down on the bed, find the page with 'Pygmalion' on it, and quickly upturn the book on the bedside table. Every article, or documentary, or anything concerning sex dolls mentions Pygmalion, so you'd had to go and get a copy to see if it really had anything to do with them, although you had known the story vaguely already and remembered Ovid from school. You bought the translation they had in the bookshop and have come to like this passage of it particularly. It is suddenly necessary to read it to her. An incantation. It's a bit slapdash, but you want to have something to mark the occasion—to do things properly, you suppose. You're not one of those men who just jumps right in.

You return, walking back into the bathroom slowly now, letting her hear the confidence of your footsteps, offering no explanation for your absence but a smile, and you snap up a towel. Dried. She is so easy to dry.

You lay her down on the bed, thinking that she won't be too cold lying there, pale and naked, on your red sheets, and you sit on the edge alongside, the bed soughing under your weight. You pick up Ovid, find the page, glance at her, and begin. When you start reading, managing to read with the perfection only achievable when no one is watching, you feel that she is listening. It is a mere five lines, but the time it takes to read it dilates with meaning, as time does where the world is either weighted with significance or washed of it entirely. This passage has come to mean something to you and now you hear it with the ears of another simultaneously, as she might be experiencing it. Its echo. Her eyes are open, as always, and she is looking up at the ceiling in an expression of placid concentration, and you see what might be the first hint of a smile on her lips. You don't think that anything on the face itself is flickering, that muscles are twitching or the features are shifting—of course not. There is no noticeable spatial change.

But, as with the smallest of changes in a human face, it looks instead as though it is filled with emotion from the inside. She looks attentive, rather; absorbed. There is some association with those photographs of faces that psychologists (or psychologists in films at any rate) show to patients, where the patient's reading of an ambiguous expression is meant to betray something about their own emotional state. But you don't pursue or really address the thought entirely, and it flits away.

You finish reading and turn to look at her again. She appears mid-ships pleased and impatient, such is her desire for the moment to come. You stand up and walk to the window, looking out. Beyond the pane, across the street, in a cranny between the tiles of the roof opposite and a dormer window, two pigeons strut. One is in front of the other, and bends her neck back, all the way, to gobble at the beak of her partner. He dips down to clack his beak against hers in response and they snap, staccato, in perfect coordination, before her head bobs back up to upright in rewind. The whole kiss happens so quickly that one might miss it. The tempo of their lives is so much more fleet. Eyes glaze into the middle distance. Birds strut out-of-focus. Your arms are clasped behind your back and you press your groin against the radiator beneath the window sill, feeling its warmth rise to your chest, and the heat blending with your excitement produces a weak feeling as though you are going to pee. You ponder what you are about to do. With your back to her you gasp the word "fuck" to yourself, relatively inaudibly. Then, after a few seconds, you turn around, framed, elegantly you would hope, in her peripheral vision by the pale grey London sunlight as she lies there. Made to wait.

You lie next to her on the bed, and she is bobbed and buoyed as you sidle nearer on the mattress, the surface tension of its fibres and the air in its stuffing bringing it halfway to liquid. You look at her. You touch her chin with a finger, as they do in films, to turn her face towards you. Then you lie still a minute—you must appear calm, to her, but anxiety comes over you intermittently with a trance-like throb, all in a reflex designed to prepare you for action but which itself overwhelms. How poorly made. You haven't been naked in front of anyone for a while. And this time it involves acknowledging something else too.

You take her hand, then, and press it to your chest, to where your heart is, to still its beating. You want to get her used to you, you tell yourself—for she might be nervous. It is the first time for you, having sex with her, but she has never had sex at all, with anyone. To take care of someone else is often the best way of taking care of oneself, and in playing her experienced guide you find yourself more calm—yet with the dream logic of play her hand on your chest is still placed there to look after you. She's comforter and comforted. You've always yearned for this from women—an infantilising curatorial love. Here it is.

You undo the cuffs of your linen shirt, which fall open easily. The speed of this, and that at which you unfasten the front buttons, take the shirt off, and then kick off your jeans, comes upon you rather quickly, and you notice too late that you have taken off your trousers before you have taken off your socks. This undressing is out of its normal order, so you hurry to pluck off the socks, but in doing so try, unusually, to pull them from the toe where you would normally roll down from the hem, and you have to exert a remarkable and inelegant amount of strength in what, it transpires, is a terrible struggle to get them off in this manner, requiring that you stretch the end of the sock remarkably far away from your toes before it begins to come away and some brown bobbles of lint roll off onto the bedspread and your toes are revealed, looking really very white.

She is there gazing up at the ceiling, but she is taking you in from the corner of her eye, you're sure of it. You're not used to this; normally undressing doesn't happen all at once until you're quite comfortable with somebody. She's that as much as anyone—some body. You try to drag off your boxers gracefully—a nearly impossible task, as you've almost reflected before but never articulated to yourself until now, and which thought you find somewhat reassuring until you remember that she's not to know how hard it is.

She may well be yours, but you're still rather ashamed. She is there built to perfection—to your very idea of perfection, no less—and a fantasy made flesh is, first of all, frightening. She lies nonchalant on the bedspread, skin not pricking goosebumps to the cold; slender attitude exquisite, not trembling or pulsing but at absolute rest. She has the smallness of the gymnast or the dancer—the perfection of her proportions renders her much smaller; she fits so well into the world as to appear a tinier, less obtrusive part of it, with none of the spacious grotesquerie of the imperfect, the bulbous, the fat. Your skin quivers; you are aware of yourself; not with the awareness of control but with its opposite, the horrible awareness that comes with watching yourself unable to do something, like being suddenly unable to walk normally or gracefully when you know that someone is watching your gait. Your short penis, which you wish was bigger but feel you deserve, is violently hard, with your nerves as much as despite them.

Shame runs through you as you look at her, your chest heaving with her little hand on top of it—a hand which you then take and press to your penis, where the way her hand doesn't go for it, grasp it, speaks of her nerves, or coldness, or repulsed excitement, or a mixture of these. Your shame struggles, turns, as is the wont of shame, to resentment, and a kind of defiance. Fuck her. She's a doll. You made her this way. You can't, surely, be so weak and pathetic as to be nervous about her opinion—as though she had one. You bought her. This, your body and behaviour, is just how you are and she will love you for it—she is what you make her. And now, you notice, it's her who is a little scared, but tender, wanting you. You show her your penis—half introducing her to it (she's scared), half imagining that she is making a move on you (she's forward). As with a word in the half-silence of the page, in the imagination one doesn't have to choose just a single enunciation to the exclusion of all others. As with the interpretation of a note on a score, she isn't concretised in voice.

Still, it is hard to touch her. As one wouldn't want to fuck a painting, so she is shockingly immaculate, inviolate to touch. With every meeting of your used body and her unresisting form you must accept yourself and insist upon your desert of her. There is both an impiety to this and the wild thrill of transgression. You start slowly at first, touching her and yourself with your hands, then moving faster as you began to find the narcissism that sin exacts, and you press and rub your body against hers. She is cold and gratifying, but as the other side of the pillow is—the untouchable other side, since it is never the side you have and always colder before you touch it. You start now to revel. You push her face into your neck to kiss you there, your hand on the back of her head, and you struggle on top, letting yourself writhe and frisk to create a madness of movement in which you can't tell which is his and which is hers.

Now that she is warmed you start to explore—yet thank

god she is not hot. Were she throbbing and sliding against you and breathing steamy groaning breath in your ear, warm and perfumed, it would be too much to bear. As it is, when you bury your face in her neck and take her smell, there's enough silicone and plastic odour of fresh, factory purchase to add throes of the delight of consumer acquisition to your pleasure. You blow into her ears, having the air come back to you and her hair puff lively to reach out to your face and caress your nose, and with this she acts, interacts. Put your fingers in her ear; nip the helix and slide your teeth down to the lobule; open her mouth and pluck at her lips; they tremble in soft, palpital echo of your touch.

Yet it is only when you push into her that she really comes alive. The feel of her is so realistic. More than realistic; *idealistically* soft, the texture of what must be the perfect balance of muscle and body fat, the ideally oestrogenised softness of skin, lustre of hair. You begin to notice the details. The splay of taut tendons on her inner thighs, tensed in supple stretch, as if flexing and unflexing when you move into her and shake her legs. The spread of her belly like a dancer's, not ridged but smoothly toned, the bellybutton itself elegantly pulled taut and in exactly the right place, with no crass knot of umbilical scarring. Her tits shake gently, a tad perkier than a normal woman's, and fuller, but with just the same extreme softness and capacity for stretch of the skin around the nipples and the flesh below as you pinch them. Her lips are glossed and shiny as though wetted with the moisture of blood-filled soft-tissue flesh, rich with capillaries in bloom.

Most extraordinary of all her pussy is soft and feels wet. You'd expected it to have the frictive tug of rubber where it is in fact extraordinarily soft and squishy, and now begins to make the little wet sucking noises that fucking a real pussy does; the sliding and the tiny splash and slurp as you look into her eyes. Everything down there, the billows clutching your penis, a bit tight at first and then opening up to take you. Her eyes are looking up, not like those of real women, who turn their heads or close their eyes or have them so narrowed you can't tell if they're seeing you or not, so you can't read if they're lost in ecstasy or shutting their lids against pain or against a dream in the process of bursting—no. Her eyes were open, and open to joy.

And the more vigorously you fuck her the more lifelike still she starts to become. What had started as a flicker on her face, a near imperceptible shift of facial expressions now translates to her whole body, and as you move into her her pussy lips caress your cock, pulling out with you as you pull back, the flesh around her pudenda stretching slightly with the pull. Her legs sag up and down and tug on those tendons, or whatever they are, in the groin, and when you look back and down her feet are pointing apart and together, apart and together. Her breasts jiggle richly on her chest, her belly seems to stretch and flex and it is good to think that there isn't any shit or bile or intestine quivering around in there. You think you can feel the bottom of her buttocks clench and squeeze on your ball sack as it flaps in and tugs out down below, and her hands, one flung out to the side and the other by her waist, lie palm up in abandon. You want her around you. You want her to clutch you, pull you in, scrabble at you with nails that catch, accidentally bump teeth in eagerness, and you manipulate her into the shape of a caress. You put, first, her hands behind your head and then, when they slip back, tuck her elbows under your armpits and clamp them there. From this point, leaning heavily forward on her with the top of your chest, you throw her ankles behind you, trying to hurl her over you like a bedcover or a cloak.

Her shoulders heave and shake, not with breath but with the breath you are giving her, and you could hear yourself breathing, you were very in touch with yourself breathing, your gasps mirrored by her rustling as she moaned out in rushes against the covers, wrinkling the bedspread with her spread form. The abandon in her limbs had spread to her face, and she appeared to be opening her eyes WIDE in capital letters as her nostrils quivered and shook as though with inhaled breath. You kissed her glossy lips, smearing them to the side with yours and watching her half-pursed mouth come wider and undone, her hair shaken across her cheek as her head tilted to the side and she showed you her neck and exposed the delicate ligaments, her jugular inviting you to bite the alabaster skin, her Adam's apple just a figment of shadow playing hide and seek with the light.

The adrenaline makes you tremble and the ends of your fingers skittish, then weak, before they turn ethereal and lose sensation, and you are hot in cheek and armpit and light, dangerously light, of temple, and heavy of chest. She's so beautiful you can't hold it: you feel it somewhere in your urethra and the middle of your head that you are soon to come, as the rustling of the bedsheets gets louder and fills your world. A murmuring, pre-vocal sea, the tide of her washing against you overwhelms, drowns you out, then crashes you to shore and breaks.

When you ordered the doll you didn't expect it to be as much like living with someone as it turned out to be. You had in part assumed that it would be just another object in the house, with a relevant place in your life, to be put away and stored where it belonged; a place for everything and everything in its place. But you discovered that it's hard to have to store a human object.

Human beings don't have places, as records do on a shelf, or a saxophone does in its case; places exist to have them. She has something of the ascendancy of a pet, or a child's favourite soft toy—arranged in the bed for her comfort rather than, as you would arrange a pillow, for yours.

She does not fit anywhere and you carry her around the apartment, both to have sex with and for pride, as you might want to keep playing a piece you've just written or admiring a bit of painting or DIY just finished. There is proprietorial joy in posing her and cleaning her, like that which you take in polishing your sax. But the result of this is that, wandering around the apartment naked, or coming back home and unlocking the front door, you catch sight of her in the corner of your eye and leap out of your skin. Why is there a nude woman reclining against your record collection? Whose is the gaze locked on you as it pokes out of the bedcovers? It takes some getting used to, in particular if she has slipped out of the position you left her in so that, for a second, it looks as though there is a corpse on the living room floor with its face in the carpet and hair splayed about. One of the unnerving things about corpses must be their very silence, the fact that a body might just lie there unnoticed for minutes in a room you've been using. Having her there is like that, and in catching her in the corner of your eye your response to the incoherence of the scene is often an equally inchoate verbal ejaculation, all modulation and no substance, like "*woououer!*", before you find yourself, hand on your chest, saying "Jesus Christ", then smiling to yourself with surprise's adrenalised pleasure.

In a particular moment of reflection, as you sip tea looking out at barren trees, wondering whether they've made and stored all the energy they need for winter, their wintry fingers scraping and scratching at the sky in the wind, you can see her out of the corner of your eye and she surprises you but you do not move or react—sometimes one is dulled to surprise, and able to keep calm despite receiving something that at other times would make you jump. In you it's a kind of dreamy state that begets this ability not to start. This time you experience the emotional jolt but continue just to sip your tea, and then actively to play with her in your peripheral vision; moving your head and enjoying the blurring that softens her differences from a live woman, squinting your eyes over the steam from the mug, deliberately letting them fall out of focus to look at her through a softening blur. And as you contemplate her looking so human there it occurs to you that your peripheral vision, when you start or jump or interpret her as a person, is a tap into your subconscious. When you catch her in the corner of your eye and see her human, it's because a part of you does. Something inside you has been tricked; something takes her as alive. You are pleased for having thought of this.

She looks at you too. To begin with you feel her gaze weirdly, feel odd under it, occasionally have to turn her to face a different way. When you leave her lying on the pillow you turn her head to the side, which you prefer to having her sitting up somewhat to look out and face you, chin touching chest, or to leaving her staring upward like one in a trance. Soon, though, you come to enjoy her watching you and to react to it. You sit her on the sofa in the sitting room as you prepare your coffee, to drink with your first cigarette, and you do things more swiftly and elegantly with her there; throwing a teaspoon up into a spin and catching it again as you take it out of the drawer; putting things in the dishwasher more often, or back in the fridge, when you might otherwise have left them out; making sure you don't spend too long in bed—

having her to take care of, to take out of bed and to ready for the day, helps you to do the same. You stand taller; walk better and more purposively; suck your stomach in and use your muscles harder, when she's there watching.

You begin to make sound for her then, too. It starts with whistling to yourself more than usual. Then this expands to humming; the "tum-tee-tum-tee-tum" tune of an allegro hum done in the middle of performing an operation like making pasta, to urge yourself on and keep up a vibrant, energetic atmosphere when you're with another person. And you begin to talk to yourself. Before you might have made noises—a shout of frustration and annoyance if your computer wasn't working or a saxophone reed broke—and you certainly sang or whistled or hummed along or in improvisatory melodies when listening to music, but now, however, you start to say words. Individual adverbials first, like "yes" or "right". Decisive words. Then, on those days you're feeling particularly breezy, you start addressing her. The first occasion comes when you're tidying up (itself unusual), and in moving her from the bed to the chair in order to be able to change the sheets you say "Now, I'm just going to put you here." You'd addressed speeches to her—not written out but thought through beforehand—from when she first arrived, but they were line-reading rehearsals for what now comes unbidden. You don't remark on this, however. You don't notice, consciously, that anything is different.

Whereas alone you had pissed with relative silence against the enamel back of the bowl of the loo, now if she is in the next room you direct your stream into the water where it falls and clatters heavily. This has to do with showing off, but you've never done it with a real woman. You find yourself listening for what she hears. As you brush your teeth: the buzz of the electric toothbrush and its modulations in pitch and volume as you scrub it across your teeth and open and close your mouth; an intricate sonic landscape. The rising tone of a glass being filled with water at the bathroom tap: moving from an exact E2 almost an octave to what you pitch as a D. Your coughing, and grunting, and creaking on chairs and floorboards: the rustling acoustic of your existence, constantly crackling into sound and motion whereas she sits still and so often silent. She was able to be quiet, when others make so much unmelodious noise.

She begins to take on character. The attitudes she strikes in repose, afforded by the way she is made, and her constant milky nudity make her resemble a dreamy Olympia. Her body language is most often that of languorous abandon, limbs flung wide, neck arched back, hair falling carelessly about her face, eyes glazed into the middle distance at a fine point in air, lost in a post-coital reverie of blankness. She is naturally longing, stretched out like a cat in the sun; a mixture of desire and satiety. At other times she's lying in bed, on top of the blankets, shoulders raised. A long, long shrug at the world, shirking off its weight and responsibility, affecting a bored, existential smirk, but appearing ready to burst into joyful and self-mocking laughter, to drop the shoulders and admit, when you come to tickle her, that it was only a pose and she was only pretending.

You take a great deal of particular pleasure in her accidental movements, or those which appear to be accidental. Sometimes, as you fuck her vigorously, her arm is shaken so her palm rubs across one of her tits and it looks as if she's fondling it, caressing herself and enjoying her own attractiveness. At others, if you jostle her particularly hard in missionary or pull her abdomen towards you in jerks, her waist between your hands, holding her onto you as a puppet on your cock, and her in half-bridge leaning back against the bed—at such moments the arm falls up sometimes, the back of her hand pressed to her cheek or temple as though to take her temperature or to make the swooning motion that has come, in popular culture, to signify a loss of control or consciousness; abandonment to pleasure or heat or shock; loss of selfhood at the hands of a male. The fingers left to curl uncontrolled, only part-contracted—their lack of muscular precision indicating the languor of the mood. No gesture could be more useless. That's no doubt the point. And then if you're fucking her with you both sitting up, legs encircling each other that way, and unless you grasp a handful of her hair in your fist at the back of her neck—her head falls forwards and butts yours. But gradually you find the knack of fucking her slowly, letting the hair slip through your fist and shaking her just enough that her forehead merely topples gently to meet yours and stays there, with the pressing together of heads that people do to symbolise making their minds meet—footballers in celebration and lovers in softcore porn particularly.

You begin to invest some of her movements with superstition. You play 'she loves me, she loves me not' with whether she slumps to your side or the other if you sit down next to her hard on the sofa. When her arm falls off the back of it and onto your shoulders she's expressing herself, as when you sit her on the floor and she slumps backwards to lie sprawling. You even enjoy it—especially enjoy it—when her movements don't make contextual sense, because they have more personality that way. Thus sometimes, left to look at you on a chair, her head falls to the side and she eyes you askance, as if you've done something odd or she's inspecting you as a specimen. You imagine her witty observations on what you're doing, then: "Polishing your instrument again, are we?" as you clean the saxophone. "You're not still doing the dishes are you? First we couldn't pay. Now we'll never be allowed to leave this place if you don't hurry up!" Once or twice you catch yourself whispering, or opening and closing your mouth around her comments, gaping like a goldfish to yourself, your chin pressed against your shirt as you look down and stir your coffee. To begin with you were just guessing what she *might* say, but soon you start to feel you know what she *would* say—what she is saying. But still you don't yet hear her voice, and the words arrive to you without attendant timbre and intonation, most of the meaning abstracted and lost. Because, for you, tone's not just an addendum of speech but the main part of meaning. You can't yet hear her tone.

Her throes of modesty and her throes of exuberance in nudity are as temperamental as woman. For whilst most often she lies in languorous abandon, at other moments you find her face down on the bed or rolled up in the covers, hiding from you, and you're a bit shocked—you don't remember having left her like that. Sometimes she has moods, and won't look at you; you turn to her and her head is facing the other way on the pillow. Others, you open your eyes in the middle of the night and she's been watching you as you sleep, only feigning to hide from behind the hair that she has allowed to flop over her face—which she could even have affected on purpose, in fact; deliberately acting cute.

But the part of her that can never pretend is her pussy. With her you never worry whether you can get it up, whether the position is good for her or if you are crushing her or lying on her awkwardly. Her pussy tells you that she always wants you—always will want you. Her pussy is always open—it is different to a real woman's that way, and is clearly something they haven't managed to get exactly right yet. Instead of the lips closing most of the time, like a piece of sutured flesh, as it is on a real woman, and which you have to, in some cases, kind of find your way through with saliva on your fingers until you meet the wetness inside and can draw it out—instead of this her lips are always open, spread to the sides so you can see the taut flesh of the interior—the bits of the vestibule that resemble stretched gums, or have something of the curtained skin under a bat's wing. You like it that she is always ready to receive, always inviting you.

What you like, moreover, is that it appears to be despite herself that her pussy reveals her desire to you; that on the one hand her face is blank and emotionless, giving nothing away, feigning coyness or prudishness, acting out reserve, but on the other that secretly she wants it as much as you do, or wants it despite wanting not to want it…is even aroused by the idea of it happening somewhat against her will—in infringement of her better instincts. Some women you've been with behaved like you had to earn sex—like if you made a false move along the way or didn't do something the right way they would to disallow it to you or kick you out of bed. Others acted as though sex was a favour they were doing you—which in fact it may well have been, as some women just don't like to have sex, you believe, as much as others. And in all this you'd always wanted a woman endlessly horny, or at least open about being up for it as much as you, as much of the time. The doll doesn't have any of that prissy caprice. Her vagina shows you that she's up for it just as much as you are.

But you are closest to her, funnily enough, when you are most alone with yourself and she's just there, listening: you are closest to her when you play for her on the saxophone. You like to sit her on a white wooden chair that your grandfather made.

It's sized for a child and has his initials on the back. Then you sit opposite, and warm the instrument between your legs before you play. Improvising on the sax, for you, is like stepping out of your front door. At first the streets are yours; they are the ones you see from your window every day; they begin with patterns and melodies you know well. You follow a regular stroll, a pavement every surface eccentricity of which you know: each pothole filled in with bitumen that swells proud above the flagstones; the long esker the bus has made on the road, rumpling the tarmac into a pleat under its weight on hot days; the wobbly paving stone that splashes a remarkably large gout of water when you step on it after rain. It's a funny kind of memory—you couldn't call up or draw the details of the pavement were they not in front of you, but you recognise the cracks when they're there to be recalled. You would know if something changed. As you blow sax you walk, most often, down one of these routes first.

And then, as you take a specific route away from home, things become a bit less familiar. You've walked this way before, you know it still, but whilst there are things you recognise there are now new things to notice which you hadn't seen before; a trill of the fencework, the volutes below a clock on the wall, a gargoyle next to a chimney stack. A path that is red brick where you'd remembered grey flags. The lightning-strike crack all through the perpend of a façade. And then—and this must happen all at once—you are somewhere you have never been. If you turn around you can still see streets that you know; the path you find yourself on hasn't changed in character; it is still contiguous with the environs through which you have been strolling; but it is new. A new flight of notes; a stone staircase rising. A spray of magnolia flowers drooping suddenly over the wall; a trill. A red, self-contented post box; a slow, low modulation. Your foot in the soft mulch of a flowerbed; a sudden two-tone bend. A scale played out of order; ivy's fingers scaling a wall.

You've strolled away from home but, this time, after walking for a while you catch something out of the corner of your eye that seems familiar. A half-remembered arrangement of colour; a scrap of a Mondrian or a Rothko you know; a fragment of Kandinsky you've seen before, that you remember in abstract: but the lines and the colours. You don't yet remember the things themselves, just the harmony between them and their proportions to each other; their relationships, and not what they are. It is yet but the ghost of lost memory.

But you do know what it is that you are looking for. It's something that you've played before, something you've been trying to recapture for a while, in fact. There was a night at Ronnie's, a night where you played this thirty-two bar phrase, your turn to solo, and you blew what you considered a fantastic melody, a skein of rhythm and tune, a coruscating song that came out blown complete. You have tried to grasp and reach out for it over the months since but it had vanished entirely from view. And now you've found the start of the thread of it again; the end of the string on the path.

As yet, however, it's still on the edge of your consciousness, in the corner of your eye. You have to creep up on it sideways, lest you break it or scare it away by looking at it too suddenly. It has all the fragility of just-glimpsed morning dreams, and you don't want to blow it into air, like something writ in smoke. The need to remember it has the same sense of urgency of all forgotten things—even those which, when you do finally recall them, turn out to be unimportant—and at times this urgency itself can intrude upon your mental space and banish the memory. In grasping for it too quickly you can unravel it, lose it forever but for the vaguest residue left behind, or until chance throws something from the dream into your lap later in the day and you can pick up its thread from another, ravelled end. But you have become expert in getting such butterflies to land on you: just stay completely still and hope it stays for all your trembling.

And it's ok because this isn't a dream—only partway to one—and because it's not so much remembering as inventing the piece again; letting your hands and lips follow it; your lungs follow it; letting every part of you that's not *you* remember. Your fingers start to find the once-run way, you begin to trace the tune like braille, to push your lips forward as though to pronounce a word, to slip your breath back into this once-blown cadence. And, as you do so, beneath the noise of the saxophone, you hear her breathe out, like the air leaving a pillow, like a wisp of steamy vapour escaping a teapot as it sits cooling on the table, too eager to oblige. Four bars more. You hear her breathe in, like the air entering an envelope when you open it—not the sound of the paper tearing and rustling, just the sound of the air. Surely it is the keys of the saxophone, coming unstuck—a pursed whisper at the corner of your mouth—the blankets in the bed breathed open by the wind—surely she does not breathe. She exhales, louder this time, then makes a hum of relaxed agreement, as though taking a sip of something delicious or relaxing down in her chair, "mmm."

Quite suddenly the whole form of the tune becomes present before you, and you are back in Ronnie's, forehead sweating from the lights and the audience nearly invisible in the darker, red banks of seats around. But what truly comes back to you as you riff on the tune mournfully, becoming master of it now, having found it out within yourself and blown it out, is a corner of memory in the corner of that room—something you'd forgotten about, to the extent you didn't even know you'd forgotten it, but which this end of the tune has brought back with the tail end of that night; something that happened after the gig.

The lights are up in the auditorium, the stage lights off, creating once again an even plane between spectator and performer—there is no longer the ascendancy of the light and height of a stage in performance, the tension where you are all they can see for the darkness and you can see nothing of them for the light. Now the illumination is even, and things have their colours again. The drunkenness, the permissiveness of shadows is gone and you can see, trodden into the red carpet, a black disc of chewing gum which was not there before.

You are standing next the corner of the stage, your saxophone already in its case, and you are talking to Ray, the drummer, as he crouches next to the kit and packs away his cymbals—when a racy American (from New York, you wondered?), drunk from too many gin martinis, comes over and starts talking, beginning as though you were already mid-conversation in the way Americans do. She wants to tell you, and the band, and anyone who'll listen, about her husband and his love of jazz and playing jazz electric guitar. She is small, oddly swarthy, with a bob of straight black hair and little eyes which look as though they should have glasses. Her conversational style is almost entirely oblique; not concerned with dialogue but merely with broadcasting—childless, you imagine this woman, but the sort who could otherwise be one of a pair of housewives talking at each other, each about their own child's feats and misdemeanours.

But with this woman, just behind her, is her friend. A striking blonde, with thin legs in black tights which ought to be too young for her but aren't, very sexy with a long nose and this slightly curled blonde hair at shoulder length, and very thin fingers with gold rings holding a glass of a sparkling wine. She is staring at you with these dreamy, green or blue Gene Wilder eyes. There is a particularly dorky or otherworldly expression to those fingers as if she isn't much used to interacting with the hard objects of the world. Like a child she has the stem of the glass pinched, or rather pressed between the very pads of her fingers and thumb whereas most adults have learnt that this is precarious and relies too much on friction, holding it instead in the crook of the first joint of the index finger, if not at the middle phalanx or even further down. When she is introduced by her companion she turns out to be called 'Fizzy'. "Why are you called Fizzy?" the drummer, Ray, calls out from amongst his kit on the stage. "She's called Francis Wilson" her friend immediately answers, exclaiming breathlessly for her as Fizzy stares ahead with a small smile turning up the corners of her lips and eyes, "but we call her 'Fizzy' because she's got the shakes, so when she holds a glass of something sparkling it gets all fizzy." And the loud friend breaks into cackles.

You can't remember anything specific that Fizzy said but you recall her voice, and with your musician's ear can recreate it in imagination. And, as you remember, it comes at once with the realisation that hers is the voice of your doll; not even the realisation, but the certainty, the way that you just know things—that somebody is part someone and part someone else, or that you are in your grandparents' house, or have murdered somebody—in dreams. When Fizzy speaks—when your doll speaks—her voice has a Midwest quietude, the near-English pronunciation of the cultured woman from Missouri (or 'Missoura', as you know one says if really familiar with the place). It has the part-trendy part-geeky twang of the college sophomore, the liberal arts college sophisticate; the borderline self-conscious nasality of a clever girl who probably summers in Nantucket.

To your fine auditory attention it is easy to summon up remembered voices. Their ranges, cadences, trills; their tones and vibrato and modulations; their tempos and rhythms and timbres. Hers occasionally squeaks a "yeah", but despite its twang it is usually relatively low. It has this chuckle, a boyish humming laugh that swells up cheekily and bursts through the lips, which she seems to lose some control over and which quaver a bit, then, barely open. It is relaxed, sing-song, with the open, long, flat vowels of the Midwest and the upper middle class clipping of the crisp consonants. It is laid-back but scholarly, easygoing but serious. Its kind, amused gentility could easily be mistaken for stupidity, yet it is anything but; it's just a supple voice. This is the voice of your doll.

You won't forget this piece now, now that you've walked the path a second time. And you begin to have conversations, after that, you and your doll. Her voice was toneless before, but now it is full, fully-formed, and alive. Previously you had spoken to the doll, but now she begins to speak to you.

"You know, you're what I want in a woman" you say to her.

"What do you mean?"

"Well, there's something quiet about you. Other people make so much unmelodious noise."

"It's not surprising that I'm quiet. Though I'm *very* careful not to bother you" she says, with a glint of irony that you almost miss.

You make a half-chuckle grunt in your throat.

"It's not just that" you tell her. "I mean, that's more like a small part of what it is, part of the whole way you are. Like, with my other girlfriends I'd always felt that I was with someone, all the time, having to be someone." A smile shines in her eyes, which gawp a tad wide and goofy. "With you I feel alone, like I can just be myself."

"You can. I like you J."

In response to this you turn half away from her on the bed. Half-hiding a blush? Half-pretending to? You pause.

"When I speak to you like this I can find a fluency I don't really have in real life. Like giving imaginary stirring speeches to yourself as a child, playing at the end of the garden, and your eyes pricking at your own rhetoric. I can think way down deep into myself with you. Like…even what I just said there, articulating that, it came out so clearly. But it also would have been hard to do that without you, I mean, totally by myself."

"I know what you mean. I can too. What I say always seems to fit right into place with you."

"Yeah. You know, in a way you're the most beautiful woman I've ever been with. It's like…like…that's sort of odd to say, but there isn't anything about you that I don't like. You don't have some kind of wonky toes, or thick knees, or anything like that. And you don't do anything I don't like. You don't warm your cold feet against me, or always want to borrow my sweater, or put the toilet paper on the holder with the end facing inwards not outwards. You don't get angry if I watch a film without you."

"Well, those things aren't that big a deal."

"I know. I know. You're right I guess."

"Yeah. But I'm glad you like that about me."

"Yeah, I don't feel so alone."

Another time, you're lying on the bed next to each other, holding hands. "You know one of the things I love about you?" you ask.

"Well, you never stop telling me" she says wryly, her voice smiling.

You laugh. "Well maybe I won't this time then, if it's getting too much."

"No please…I didn't mean it like that…of course I want to hear"

You laugh again. "Oh darling, don't worry, *I* didn't mean it like that. I was only teasing."

Her reply is a look of pleasure and relief.

"What I was going to say is that one of the great things about you is that you don't have any exes. At least, none that I know of…"

"I don't" she says seriously.

"Yeah. Well. Women seem to have these ubiquitous tales of horrible ex-boyfriends. Marge, for example, told me about one she'd lived with. And how, after they'd been quarrelling, he woke her up from a nap by throwing an empty suitcase on her. Or my one at university, even, when we were eighteen, had one where her boyfriend had come drunk to her house and ripped her clothes off and hit her in the face. Jeez, I haven't thought of that one for a while. She hit him back, she said. They must only have been seventeen. Is that more or less cruel? Imagine what that must have been like. I haven't thought about it for, probably, a decade. Now it seems almost funny, especially her hitting him back, and two young teenagers acting out such scenes, but back then it freaked me and I couldn't stop thinking about it. Feeling as though I had to stop it happening, and also that, to be telling it to me, she must have liked something about it, that a part of her had been, like, claimed by this chap."

"I bet you imagine them way worse than what they were though."

"Yeah. Yeah, I'm sure you're right. I probably thought about them more than the girls did. And you just get fixed with an image in your head, really vague, like an empty suitcase with the zip undone bouncing on the bed, and the face awakening in shock with eyes wide to work out what's going on, and then it becomes this whole thing."

"Right. Probably it wouldn't have been so bad at all—even funny—if you'd actually been there."

"Yeah that's true. Yeah, I think you're right."

"Yeah."

You both pause, lying next to her on the covers of your bed, you clothed, her naked, holding hands but staring up at the ceiling.

After a while a thought comes to you. It's one of those thoughts you don't think you could have had if she wasn't there.

"There must be some kind of instinct to talk about your exes to your new partner; I can't imagine that those girls just went around telling everyone about it."

"Mm, you're right."

"I wonder what the instinct is to do that. Some kind of sharing, like it's a big part of their history and they want to share it with you, or a kind of exorcism, or guilt at it having happened… at having let themselves be involved in something like that. Or wanting approval for how they acted…or checking that you think the same about relationships…or…or maybe even to show the other person how they can be valued by others, even to the point of fury or hurt…to show how interesting and complex they are and maybe even to make their new partner jealous."

"Yeah. Or just a kind of sympathy, maybe too. You know? Like, they're still shocked that it happened and want you to show them that they're still alright. That you still love them. And maybe all the other stuff about making you jealous and making a story of whatever happened is just another way of dealing with it. Telling themselves that it makes them more complex, when actually it was just, like, a little shameful."

"God, you're so right."

You pause and stare at the ceiling again.

"Jeez, I've been doing it myself just now."

You can feel her smile next to you. You both look at the ceiling. Then you smile too.

After a while she says "You need someone new. Forget all those old ghosts."

"That's why I've got you" you reply immediately.

You can't imagine her expression.

Like other lovers, you go over your origin story, the fable of your meeting, rubbing it like a coin which you scour blank even as you shine its face. "What did you think of me when I first opened the box?" you ask her.

"Oh my god" she says, shocked at the question, "I was so frightened."

"Frightened?" you say, laughing.

"Yeah! I was terrified. I had no idea who you were, or what was happening…and then when you kissed me…"

"…yes?"

"It was so overwhelming. I…I didn't know what to think."

"I loved it when I first saw you" you tell her. "There was something in your eyes I liked so much."

"Oh, yeah?" she says, high and hopefully.

"Yeah. They're what I remember best. Such a light blue when I opened the crate they looked like you could just blow them away, just blow the colour out of them, like dust on a butterfly's wing. Not some muddy, opaque brown, but this—this clarity."

"Oh" she breathes very quietly. Then after a pause "I like you so much J."

In truth, you've gone over the memory of her arrival so much it's hard to tell if it's still real.

"I love your eyes" you say, and it's the closest you have come to speaking of love.

This was the period you were truly connected to her, and you used to lie, nights, your face buried in her bosom, eyes closed, holding her arms around you, clamping her forearms against your ears so she was holding your head to her chest. Then you would lie there and listen. What to or for you weren't sure. When you first got into the position what you listened to was her; to her flesh; and all you could hear was the rustling of everything against your ears. Then, as the movement settled, the rustling and shifting would, by a pattern of its own, abate, and you would hear your own heartbeat, pressing into your eardrums. As one does with a seashell, you would begin to listen to yourself against her. Listen harder, then, not to the beats, which fade out of countenance, but to the quieter noises between them, to the rushes of blood the beats presage and surpass, presage and surpass. A little rush, and then another. And then, quieter still, behind the rushes, behind everything, the electric hum of your own nerves; listening to your own listening—a Mobius strip of consciousness, then sleep.

Occasionally, grasping at old realities, you find yourself doing things you used to do with Marge with her. It's easy to forget the stuff that truly makes up a relationship—the little things nobody talks about—and it is only remembered again in you by her presence. You only learn how to be in a relationship—how to really be in a relationship—from your parents and from your own. You can watch as many romantic comedies as you like, listen to as many love songs, but there are certain things they don't mention, just as there are certain things your friends won't talk about—won't even be able to talk about—should you ask them.

It's the little things. Marge, lying there on the bed next to you, reading, holding her book childishly with both hands and lying flat on her back rather than on her side in a position in which you would never have been able to read yourself, her hair spread about her head on the pillow, each of its tiny complex intertwinings and interactions with itself—what she would call it being in a mess—and the way it runs across the mountains and valleys sculpted out of the pillow by her head…all of this, and the way it changes the ways the light illuminates the length of each brassy strand…even so small a sight you could find overwhelming. And her lips as she reads, totally absorbed in her book despite your gaze, are neither closed nor open. She has an inherently polite, cultured face in that her mouth doesn't fall open but rests closed; the natural embouchure of breeding. Though 'closed' doesn't describe the way her lips meet, for they are not quite touching. If she were pretending to be dead in a stage play she could still breathe through them, just, though what is left is the smallest possible apse through which she might do so. But there's nothing, nothing tense at all about the lips, or in her face. You feel like you're watching her when she's alone.

And, because you can't resist it, because you're only human, because this moment of being overwhelmed and awed by her quiet beauty and her nut brown pupils and wide, dilated eyes is still not something you, being human, can concentrate on for long, as one can't concentrate on anything but the perpetual next for long…because of this, you lean over very rapidly, ducking under her book, and fasten your lips on the end of her slender nose, both kissing it and holding it.

You are so, so close up to her face, and there has been a funny moment of silence between you two as you have moved to complete this action and she has reacted, or rather failed to react, spellbound and frozen by shock and not sure what was going on and not wanting, probably, to move during your swift approach in case she might butt you and hurt you or herself, so you have found yourselves in this position in a silence only punctuated by the rustling of fabric and her beginning to move her book then stopping. Then you see her eyes widen, so so close to your own, and you widen yours mock-monstrously in return, and you hear her lips open with her gasp of mock outrage, and then she squeals through a smile "Nooooo!"

"-se" you add to her exclamation, letting go the kiss. "Nose."

The most charming thing about doing this to Marge was that she never learned, and never stopped squealing "nooo!" automatically. It was such an organic response, emerging naturally in the panic of the moment, and each time you added the "zzz" of "nose" as though correcting her it was funny afresh—funnier, even, because she had given you the opportunity to make the joke again. You try to play this game with the doll. Of course it doesn't work without the actual cry for you to answer and complete. Her expression stays the same.

A few days after trying this, at a time when you feel together with the doll to the extent that it is hard to leave her, you get three days of session work with a singer at Angel Studios in Islington. They need a saxophonist. You get the call up from Solomon, who is that rare thing: a sound engineer who's also a fixer. As enervating as it might be you have to stay in Solomon's good books. You like the guy, he's just so…familiar.

It is the last day of recording. Grant is there on trumpet. He's next to you, as he often is at such sessions, a Perspex sheet set between you. All morning he's been making crazy faces at you just before the takes; sex faces, or faces where he rolls his eyes up into the top of his head and opens his mouth and shakes like someone possessed, sometimes bringing up his hand in a fist with his index and little fingers pointed up to make the sign of the horns. He's an insanely brilliant and technical trumpet player but, unless you're in the right mood, insufferable in person for more than ten minutes. During breaks he likes to make you listen to his transposition of some insane Robert Fripp guitar solo to the trumpet, or another piece of bizarre prog-rock he's been pointlessly perfecting. He's probably about twenty years older than you, and he's also pretty large; a big Scottish man with stringy but naturally taut looking musculature and a barrel chest. He has a pale complexion and is red cheeked in a way that is almost comically cherubic, but he's also balding, with wisps of flaxen-grey hair on the top of his head that float around hilariously when he plays. You think he might be a bit autistic, but he's in general an energetic and winning (if unpredictable) presence, who is at least deeply into his craft.

This is more than can be said for the singer. It's taken three days to record two jazz numbers for this label-baby, who takes an hour each morning to get the mix right in her headphones, plastering everything in reverb when she's going to get the

Melodyne treatment from Solomon in post-production anyway and be never the wiser. By the afternoon of the last day you've reached a kind of frustrated apathy.

"Jesus H Christ" says Grant in his loud Scots voice as soon as you have stepped outside the front of the building and are walking round to the back on a break in the afternoon. "That little pop tart strumpet. That little…cunt!" he says the word with the explosive relish of a schoolboy being knowingly naughty, and immediately follows it with too-loud open-mouthed laughter, which he emits staring at you and which you never know if you should join with an inevitably bathetic, artificial chuckle, or merely answer by making a smile that might look patronising. The sound he makes is a cackle that sounds the way laughter is written: "Ah-ahahahahah."

"Uuuugh" you reply, in mingled complaint and relief. Ray the drummer and Andy the bassist are walking just behind you two as you open the wooden gate that leads down the side alley to the building's back garden, and you overhear one of them saying something annoyed and hushed with "fuck" in it.

"Did you hear her miss out the second A and come storming in with the bridge?" Grant has turned suddenly earnest, nearly downcast. "Who the fuck does that? It's such incompetence. It's like, have some professional respect, you know?"

"I know" you reply, shaking your head and rolling a cigarette as you all walk across the back lot towards the wooden table bench, you and Grant in front, Andy and Ray behind. It's a grey but temperate London afternoon.

"Jesus Christ. I wanted to fucking wallop her" Grant says.

"And what were those hand signals at the end?" you join in, "She kept signalling round and round for turnarounds, surely, but then just went ploughing on straight into the buffers."

"Ohh Jesus. Don't get me started."

Andy, also somewhat of a schoolboy in this environment, chips in from behind "I've got hand signals for her" and sticks his hand, middle finger upraised, over the shoulders of you and Grant from behind so you can see it in front of you.

Grant gets excited by this and, not to be outdone, stops and turns around, blocking the path of Ray and Andy and forcing them to halt, at which you also pause out of politeness, and, jutting out his jaw so his bottom teeth bite his upper lip, squatting bow-legged like a spider, he pretends to throttle the singer for a second, miming shaking her by the neck, then suddenly bellowing laughter as he swears at her imaginary place in the air with both middle fingers, and the others chuckle too.

"Oi Andy, can I borrow a schnoot?" he says as you arrive at the table. He means a cigarette.

The break bench is in a back lot area of dirt relieved by patchy grass and the occasional weed. It is partially shaded by a big tree that looks like a London plane. Around the bench the ground has been worn completely free of grass to hard earth, but is spotted with beer bottle tops, small pieces of plastic, and cigarette butts despite the big terracotta dish in the middle of the table—in which so many filters have been stubbed it resembles the Giant's Causeway.

Ray sits down while Andy is giving Grant a cigarette and they light up. You light your own roll-up with a trembling hand, and then say "Guys I'll be right there, I've just got to call the girlfriend."

This comes out all in one breath from too much mental rehearsal, and it seems to you that it must have been made a nonsense by this arrhythmia, but the others barely register it, as if you have said something not only unremarkable but quite inconsequential. You had, on the walk along the path, been thinking the words and how you might say them, but you hadn't made any decision until they just slipped out, a vague idea suddenly made solid in a second's inspiration. You walk off until you are nine or ten metres away to stand by the metal fronting of a garage or bike shed, where you will be just on the edge of earshot. This is as close as the game can get to others; just on the outskirts of conversation, the edges of the heard, a few snatched words, a relationship implied rather than discussed, accepted as another part of the uninvestigated ephemera of all the social relationships of others: their girlfriends, husbands, dogs, jobs, holidays, all of it. You're trying to paint yourself into the background, have her a flicker of colour at the back of the consciousnesses of your co-workers. You know, too, that these people won't ask you questions afterwards. You don't have that kind of relationship, and it wouldn't be cool.

So, with shaky breath, you call your home phone. It rings, and rings, and then there is the solemn beep.

"Hello?" you say down the line.

(The response is a garbled noise from the end, the smatterings of a voice dissected by signal.)

"Hello darling, are you there? Can you hear me?"

("Darling?" comes the reply.)

"Hello!"

("Oh ya. Hey." It is her. It is the doll.)

"Hey, how are you?"

("I'm good, just here chewing on a carrot." She crunches it at the other end. "How's your day going?")

"Yeah it's good thanks. Been recording with some of the guys at the studio this morning, which has been going pretty well. We laid down some good takes this morning and I'm just on break now." You're no good at acting but this comes effortlessly to you—because you're not.

("Mmm. Nice.")

"Yeah. I just thought I'd skip out to say hello—"

("Oh *hey* babe.")

"—and see how you were doing."

("I'm doing really good. Just here in the apartment. I've been looking for a new thing to do.")

"What kind of thing?"

("I'm not sure. I was wondering if you had any suggestions.")

"Mmm, something funny? Or something with action?" The thing solidifies into a film.

("I really don't know. Whatever you think is good!")

"Ok", you pronounce, considering, "let me think about it and I'll send you some ideas later."

("Ok awesome! I'm also trying to decide if I should go to my class or not.")

"Well, how do you feel?" The little details that make up a life.

("I kind of feel like I should go, you know? I haven't been for a while now.")

"Ok, that's good."

("And thingy wants me to go.")

"Oh, your friend?"

("Mmm." Crunch crunch.)

"Nice."

("But I'm super tired from yesterday.")

"Yeah, we were up quite late."

("Yeah.")

"Well, there's one every day, right?"

("Yeah, every weekday at six.")

"Well I suggest you skip it today and go tomorrow instead when you'll really feel like it and be less tired."

("Ok! Yeah. That's a good decision.")

"Right?"

("Totally. So…mmm…what do you want for dinner?")

"Oh, anything darling. Whatever you want to make."

("Ok, I'll make something nice.")

Reality sets in.

"Oh wait, but…I might have to stay out a bit with the boys." You look over to see if they have heard, providing the opportunity for a waggish raise of the eyebrows or a comical nod. Grant is jabbing in the direction of Andy with his cigarette, and they are quite oblivious.

("Mmmm" she says in realisation or remembrance, with her mouth full of carrot.)

"Yeah, I'll let you know how it goes, but I might be back late."

("Oh ok darling. Well I'll just be here.")

"Ok great. Well I'll let you know but don't wait up or anything." Solomon has emerged from the back door, portly in a worn burgundy cardigan and ill-fitting corduroys, and looks around myopically for a second before he makes you out.

("I won't…but I might have a surprise for you when you get home…") Solomon catches sight of you and waves, then starts beckoning at you to come in.

"What! […] What is it?" You hold up a raised index finger at Solomon. One minute.

("Can't tell.")

"No. You're a darling."

She giggles at the other end of the line.

"But you must tell me. What is it."

("Mm mm" she says, shaking her head, you are sure.)

"Urh. Dammit. Well, I can't wait. I'll try to come home early."

("Anytime darling. I'm just gonna be here.")

"Ok. I love you."

("I love you too. Bye babe.")

(And the line goes dead. She's quite flippant with hanging up like that, as though she is too coy and shy for the extended protocol of formulaic goodbyes and prefers to finish abruptly rather than risk any politic exchange of formalities or attestations. You find it charming.)

Solomon is waiting for you at the back door, eyes cast down to the concrete stoop in front of him, in a kind of suspended animation as he waits. Fuck, what does he want to show you now? As you hang up the phone and start walking over he looks up, waving a pudgy, leathery hand. "Jacob!" he calls out, pronouncing it 'Ya'aqov.' "Come! I have something to show you."

You smile awkwardly and walk towards him. As you pass the break bench Andy, as if to say 'What a treat!', gives you a melodramatic wink in camaraderie regarding Solomon, then says "How was the girlfriend mate?"

"Better than this'll be" you say quietly in passing. Solomon is looking up at you eagerly and fixedly with his wet eyes, and an unabashed, radiant smile on his lips.

"Come, come Ya'aqov" he says as you approach the back door of the building, and squeezes your shoulder hard as he manoeuvres you through the door alongside him. He's your height but overweight, with thick forearms and a kind of wobbly, clutching strength. He has a distinct smell, Solomon—homely and dusty, of leather and mothballs and sweetmeats and sound equipment. You reckon he's about fifty, possibly older. He treats you with a conspiratorial air which you find suffocating, as well as tragically embarrassing in front of the others, but there is also a great part of you that both pities and—strange as it is to say—loves this man. It's a resentful love, mingled with a lot of irritation, as well as guilt at being irritated and at needing to mock him behind his back with the others. But whereas most of these chats with him are grating, boring in the way only inflicted activity can be, this attachment gives rise to moments of clarity and complete relaxation with Solomon that you rarely have with anyone else. You just wish he wasn't so self-satisfied and sure of your attention in a way that feels like an imposition on your adulthood, as though you were in fact a child; something you'd tried to escape.

"How is your mother?" he asks on the way though the corridor.

"I think she's fine."

"Good—" he pauses as if about to ask another question, but seems to restrain himself: "good."

Breathing heavily he ushers you into his little back room, full of tumbling piles of vinyl and books and pieces of electronic equipment in various states of disassembly. There is a menorah on the sill of the small wooden window casement, and next to it a blood-red-flowering plant. He has wax worth a fortune just scattered around, slip cases signed by artists, producers, legends he has worked with, and it's just getting bent in corners, priceless original cuts in lacquer and metal masters piled on top of toolboxes. But whilst the rest of the room is in disarray the space behind Solomon's desk is kept immaculate, occupied by a 1960s Hugh Spencer Project G Clairtone: a long rosewood cabinet suspended about a foot from the ground by its metal stand, and with a built-in turntable and speakers in the shape of black, slipperily reflective globes attached by floating brackets on either side. Fewer than four hundred Project G Clairtones were ever made, and the prestigious models are usually named individually; Solomon's is called the Regina T4. Above it, mounted on the back wall, are more modern speakers it can also play through, but you and Solomon both prefer the originals.

"I think you will like this. I want to show you my new pickup." Solomon bustles behind the desk. He flaps a hand in your direction without looking, waving you into a leather chair.

"I had a friend in Japan make for me this moving-coil mono cartridge. Most moving coil is not good, but at its best, it is the best." He looks at you and you raise your eyebrows to display interest, and nod in agreement. Solomon is opening the top of the credenza as he talks. "The cartridge on this is from African Blackwood. Most resonant." You look up at the window as a sycamore fruit loosed by the wind bumps into it. He has whipped out a record from its sleeve and is holding it up for a second in your direction, but as you turn to look he has already put it down and you don't see what it is.

"This Miles is so much better in original mono, you know. The hard panning on the stereo version is not good, not good." He drops the disc and lifts the automatic arm of the turntable with the touch of a button. A block of wood so dark and polished that it seems to take in the light and give it out more slowly falls onto the disc, the ideally violent proboscis of its needle seeming a necessary acumination of its beauty into sheer reflection.

"This is how it is meant to sound. Listen."

The needle snakes on the vinyl, revealing the difference in

its shape from a perfect disc that you can never make out by eye. By the time the announcer has said "My name is Mort Fega" you know what the record is: *My Funny Valentine: Miles Davis in Concert* (1965). By the time the applause for Mort's intro fades out, you are already gone, man.

Your first date with Marge contained a moment of inevitability like nothing you have ever experienced, before or since. It is simple to state: a Miles Davis record came on in the wine bar. You told her a jazz anecdote. In that moment, you knew you had become bound to kiss her. It sounds, when stated thus with retrospect's casual ease, when fate is laid out to memory like clothes before a king, mundane. But at the time the kiss was held so closely inside the anecdote— and yet which kiss had not and would not yet come—that it was as though you had begun to play a record spinning inwards, had set the needle down with all that black space certainly to be sounded. It makes a two syllable thud-slide. Begin.

It was winter. You met in a wine bar near Temple. She had: her hair cut in a blonde bob; a quizzical expression that looked, at first blush, innocent, but which you came later to know had its own irony; a nose somewhere between snub and ski-jump, but not small and somewhat broad with a slender bridge; thin, pale English lips; a large, flat mole on her left cheek beneath her eye. By the time you had sat down on the barstools she had taken off her black overcoat, and wore a grey dress buttoned all the way up to the neck, where it had a large winged 60s-style fashion collar, embroidered with white arabesques. You had both been on time.

But none of this had been very important. Nothing had been important, in fact—oh, the usual nervousness, the usual chatter, no more—until the moment itself arrived. There was no crescendo or warning, no reason to suspect that you were about to come to a knot in the grain of your life. Then, during the second glass of wine, *My Funny Valentine* came on in the bar. As soon as you hear the piano's opening notes the evening makes a key change, from just another unremarkable date to something else, and you know, quite simply, quite suddenly, everything that will follow. You've never wondered what would happen if the record hadn't come on, because it always did.

"Oh, man" you say.

Until this point the conversational turn-taking had been clunkily precise, and this is a sudden departure from direct address, dropped in a new manner. She looks at you, already excited by this mysterious new authority. "What?"

"This is one of the best jazz recordings of all time."

You're not looking at her, but down at the base of your wine glass. You turn it in your fingers by the stem, twisting. She is happy to join you in contemplation. Her hands fold in her lap on the bar stool. She looks up, a moment, as though the better to listen. You spin your glass by the stem, slowly; slowly confident; eyes with a new droop.

"So—" you begin, and pause. Miles comes in gently on the trumpet over the piano. Then abruptly hard on this upward run, hauntingly, shutting up Hancock's piano like a desk.

"What is it?" she utters quite quietly.

"It's called *My Funny Valentine*. Miles Davis. He did three recordings of it that went to vinyl in his lifetime, one in 1956, one in 1958, and one in 1965, of which this is the last." You are speaking in measures, with the jazz, as it truly begins, and you can hear your voice taking on something irresistibly compelling, conjoined in pulsion with the music, your eyes looking out of focus at your turning glass.

"They kind of map his life. The first one he made soon after he'd kicked his heroin habit. To do that he went to stay in his father's house in East St. Louis. It's cool and detached, it has calm authority; it's the sort of music Davis made during the bridge between his wild drug years and before coming into his full powers. The second one actually has John Coltrane on the sax, playing some demure background colour mainly, before he was truly known. But the last one, this one…"

You both take a moment and listen to it. Miles' trumpet grates like an impassioned machine grinding out beauty. With a smile you glance at Margaret's eyes for half a second. This woman's— and yours too, you are sure—look very wet in the low light.

"Man. This one is the Miles Davis Quintet playing at the Philharmonic Hall. Just before going onstage he'd just told the band that he'd be giving their pay for the gig away to charity. And then, in this song, he comes like a panther out in front. Coleman, who's playing the saxophone, sounds smooth behind him by contrast. He's got this ripping, tearing sound. I mean, Davis is *frightening* on this track."

You look at her and she seems excited, her front lip a little over her lower one, mouth turning up in a nervous smile.

"Hancock is creating all this jabby modal space on the piano in the background, but Miles is just *violent* out in front. It's so beautiful. He was such a bastard. His autobiography is all him beating women and doing drugs and justifying himself. But if you didn't know that and kind of hate him through this sound…I don't know."

You look up at her again and you know it has happened, and she does too. There has come, by surprise and in the middle of nothing, the moment which can't really be called a woman deciding that she will kiss you, but when it has simply happened that she will. You didn't know you owned such charm. That moment contained the rest of the night like a track to follow on the record. After that the evening had a protected inevitability like nothing else. You were just certain that it would follow like this, that it would happen this way, leading to this kiss at that moment, there, and that nothing could happen to stop it. Of course you didn't know the exact future and the details aforehand, but each moment unfolded to you with the familiar necessity of remembrance, with the sensation that it was just the inconsequent particulars coming back: ah yes, it had to be like that. It could have been no other way.

Thus. Dusk. A square. Lincoln's Inn Fields. The largest square in London. Near darkness. Her black coat. The ambiguous time between evening and night—the hollow time. Walking after the bar she pressed against you. Not holding hands. Not arm in arm. She just walked into you as if drawn, the back of her right side pressing into the front of your left through her long black coat. It was a delicious part of her elegant clumsiness, the way she moved—elegant because aloof from a consciousness of self—and you secretly thought of her later as your 'little English animal'. She walked before you and leant backwards against you. It was a pull you were both politely ignoring; almost an embarrassment of gravity, which you had brought about inevitably in the music.

Whatever you might have said to each other, if anything, between leaving the bar and what happened next is gone; the words are permanently lost. You and she were the only ones who heard them and somehow you know that neither of you remember, that no one remembers now. Nor can you remember anything of the journey between the bar and the square. Perhaps words were not said at all; perhaps the kiss followed so inevitably upon your explanation of the recordings there was in fact no interim, that one moment you were in the bar, the next you were there outside, Margaret pressed against you; a skip in the record. But you think you can feel the absence of the sentences you must have spoken. Yes—they have fallen out, but their place is there. The lingering sense of their having just sounded at the time.

What such conversation before the kiss would sound like now, if you could be there again as a silent witness, listening relieved from that internal tumult, you don't know. Perhaps you managed to preserve the impression of normal chatter despite your excitement and perhaps you did not. Whatever normal actions you were able to take occurred simply from learned automatic response, and happened somewhere very far away. Instead, the swish of her black coat and the noise it made when she pressed against you seemed to take over sound and your entire attention; the blood rising to your ears like hands clapped over them preventing any reflective presence but the now.

Odd things start to appear. You think there were pieces of merry-go-round lined up against the railings that bordered the park at the middle of the square. Horses with poles through them, rust and russet, cream coats with golden-yellow manes, things that became giant once removed from the organised circle of their fixed chase and propped up here against the black railings of the square. Soldiers' drums in painted iron; an ostrich also—you seem to make out in memory its black painted feathers flecked with still-silvery metal showing through. And segments of the painted maypole column, maybe, around which the whole thing revolved. But all is vague and dusky, the colours done in to dun by the dusk, and like a memory of childhood it only returns to you through a fog that renders uncertain whether it was truly there at all.

The diffraction that starts here spreads to what you did see— the window of the Lincoln's Inn Library. A stained-glass thing divided into panels and traversing two storeys, its sandstone masonry swelled out against the Tudor style brickwork crossed with blackened, burnt bricks in jagged latticework which made its surface vague and shifting in the darkening light. What is odd, in reflection, about this sight is that you do not know if the window was behind Margaret, over her left shoulder as she turned to face you, or whether that was impossible and it is only now that you have imagined it into that position like a Cubist painting; a vision in which perspective doesn't make sense and things no longer occlude each other but show different sides of what is ubiquitously there. Perhaps when you leant in to kiss Margaret, and her face looked up at you with eyes swimming like pools, you could see it behind her. Perhaps it was around the corner of the square entirely. But it is behind her in the recomposition now.

You had once heard a Rabbi talk of the two ancient ideals of Hebrew twilight: the dove's twilight, crepusculum of the day, and the raven's twilight, crepusculum of night. The first had surely passed, and dark had now fallen, but perhaps this was what was meant by the second. It was that point between evening and night, the minute or two between them both when sound rings first hollow, then muffled; when day's sounds and breezes abate and the winds of night have not yet struck up their breathier music. The window behind Margaret, in your memory, glisters with the last shard of light before it becomes too dark for anything to do so; it is the last thing to ring a note of brightness against the cobweb-coloured sky, and shimmers, once—the stained glass in the night the scales of a fish bright in a murk of pond—and then goes out. As the pools of Margaret's eyes go dun when you lean over to kiss her.

Then comes the moment almost too tender to touch. She looks up for the kiss, as you take back a little to look at her, and she has, from the cold, a small wipe of snot beneath her nose. The word sounds disgusting but the substance here is not, it is natural; it is just a film there as her numb nose has been running, delicately, femininely, from the cold. And she is half-embarrassed and half giving-in to her vulnerability; half-delighted by the kiss and half-indecisive about permitting it to continue given the embarrassment. For you this is quite wonderful, to have her suddenly open in such an unprepared way, and you are proud that she should have been willing to let her nose get cold for you. So looking at her and smiling you stick your tongue up and lick beneath your own nose, where you can taste a tiny slip of her salty film, then wipe beneath your own nose with the back of your hand before using your thumb to wipe under hers, towards which she has been making vague sorties with a fluttering hand, emitting the occasional nervous laugh, almost the sounds of one weeping from relief, and trying to get rid of it ineffectually without going in for a great big nose-wipe in front of you. And so you wipe beneath her nose firmly with your thumb in the way she is too embarrassed to do, then use the base of your palm again to get what's left. All the while you look with a benevolent smile into her face, and she looks up at your eyes, allowing you to do this.

And then. You had embraced her outside her coat but now you open it, undoing the three buttons one by one, and meet her lips, and as you do so you slip your hands around her waist and press your body, your overcoat also open, against hers, and the kiss leaps lither in this sudden access, you're suddenly stunningly one degree closer in sensation and she is tender, slender and spare under your grasp. You can feel her supple hips in your hands, their postural writhe and twist, and her flat breasts pressed against your chest—discs somehow of a kind with the flat, just-proud mole on her cheek.

But you can't think of this now. It is too soft and hurtful to contemplate. Instead you decide to feel, under your hand, the mane of a merry-go-round horse. Whether or not they were truly there at all you know this: the undulating surface of the cast-iron, the flaking paint at the edges of worn patches snagging your skin, how cold and thick and heavy it is, how you know it is hollow just by a kind of proprioception, without banging or knocking or shifting it—just by touch. Whether or not it was there, when it is too much to think of that kiss and your thought turns away you can still feel your hand on the merry-go-round.

Throughout the relationship with Margaret, and long since, that first date—the kiss and the anecdote—has been like a melody which you can't get out of your head. You trace and retrace it, out of order, looping wrong bits of it back into others and failing to progress, unable to move on, spinning it round and round idly for a resolution you can't recall. It has sustained your love, even when all else was painful and failing, and has its effect even now, afterwards, when you try to wash her image from your mind. It was the fable with which you cast your love, the moment with which you put a spell on yourself. Even now it seems blasphemous to disbelieve the fable's religiosity or to doubt its fated beauty— as when later on you began to wonder whether she wasn't really captivated by the Davis anecdote but whether she, too, only fantasised that she was. Even now when the relationship is over you have still never been able to look such doubts quite in the face, to consider them with the smallest degree of detachment necessary for rationality; it remains too painful. You imagine bringing it up with her, that moment, if you saw her now. You are sure that she would find it painful for a different reason—because she must think herself a fool ever to have kissed you, to have fallen for you, however much she ever truly did. It never occurs to you that it could be, for her, still painful or precious for that moment's abiding truth.

The tracks in the middle play in uncertain order. You can't recall the exact precedences of dates or occasions; in retrospect they have become interchangeable. Your grandfather had a toy he used to show you called a Myriorama. A Victorian amusement— 'for children and adults alike!' the tattered box announced exuberantly—it consisted of sixteen panels that were each segments of a landscape. A ruined Gothic tower. A waterfall. An oak. They could be placed next to each other in any order and still appear to join up, to create myriad possible landscapes—trillions, was the claim. The combination of simplicity and unfathomable possibility delighted your grandfather, as it delighted, but also somewhat frightened, you. Looking back at this time with Margaret is like arranging that toy landscape; dale can slip into valley or river; that dinner date might have been followed by cinema or by the pub with friends or by bed. Out of their broken parts you can make your own evenings to retrospect, limitless now in fantastical combinations.

But at the centre of this landscape, if its shifting skyline can be said to have a centre, there is a moment at the utmost, before which all was ascent—after which all was fall. There is a peak of ambiguity where things appear suspended of direction, a balancing point in the middle whose very significance is its uncertainty. One card stands out of the set—is it the end of one landscape or the beginning of the next? You take it out of its box—it flickers, changing faces in the memory-light, meaning something different in the midst of each narrative you might tell yourself. Look.

It was in the bric-a-brac market that the silence came to be ambiguous. It was some afternoon, perhaps you had eaten brunch together, perhaps not, and you had gone walking and come across the jumble sale. The day was bright but chill; looking down the row of square white tents opening onto the pavement the street seemed immensely long. Progress on the thoroughfare was slow. The normal tempos of walking were syncopated, slowed or interrupted by browsers moving in and out of the current on the pavement to and from the gazebos, whilst those on the pavement seemed to follow their gazes to items in the stalls. Eyes caressing, obsessively, the wares, they watched their paths forward with only their peripheral vision as if dazed. Sometimes they were snagged by a particular trinket, and as they continued to meander onward their eyes remained fixed to port or starboard, swivelling, head turning too, towards aft, as if an invisible line had caught on the knick-knack, the old boots or bicycle wheel, and the steps forward slowed. Then the tether of attention would break, the head would snap back to face front, and the gazer would skip on out of the way, mouthing apologies to those on the pavement in front of them whom they had bought to an anticipative stop in front. There are unspoken rules of pavement walking, universally the same irregardless of minor local variation, upon which the world has mutely, unanimously agreed. The form cannot reliably be rendered into words, but if you were to attempt to articulate it you might derive such tenets as: those already in a channel have right of way over those attempting to join it; don't cause another to break their stride; don't suddenly turn back the way you came. But here the protocol is abridged or forgotten, the river's usual slickness is slowed and congested, as by reeds in shallows or banks collapsing to the current from the trestle tables in the tents.

You and Marge had begun to meet with nothing planned but to see each other. You assumed unquestioningly that your company, surely, simply the fact of your being together should be enough. To imply anything else would be an insult to your love, to its absolute totality. The aimless stroll in the jumble sale is one such picturesque ramble, perhaps even consciously picturesque, and the effect of having nothing precise to do is an exquisite boredom. It being blasphemy to attend to anything else, the smell of her hair is an extraordinary miracle of which you are exhausted; there's nowhere you'd rather be and you'd rather be anywhere but here. And thus you find yourself irascible, capricious; the quiet ramble becomes an agony of ecstatic expectation; an aching, prickling delight. Illimited, each by the other, you find yourselves looking for the extraordinary in all the ordinary, as though the light which you insist exists between you could illuminate the obdurate world from within; that it too must change to delight you as a toy for a trip.

You experience, despite the tranquillity of the moment, the violence of frustrated emotion that is the paradox of boredom. You have both, perhaps, been eating delight mistaking it for happiness, and like children spoiled by sweets you cannot now desist; you two on too much manna dew hath fed. The atmosphere is too refined. Both of you, perhaps, would want to drop into seriousness, dull solemnity, but the fall seems now too far. Your worship of the other is in adoration and in hatred.

"Look at those knives. Jeez." You are looking to a cutlery set with deer hooves for handles.

"Oh no" Marge replies.

A few seconds pass, then "Rebecca lost her dog." You've met Rebecca once.

"What?" You sound shocked.

"Yeah, right?"

"The Jack Russell you talked about?"

"Yes. Jake."

"Oh shit. What happened?"

"She said she took him for a walk in the park with Rick and that he ran off, maybe chasing something. Then they were out looking for him and waiting for him for five hours and they couldn't hear him or find him and he never came back."

"Jesus."

"So awful."

"That must be very rough" you say.

And you slip into silence again, and into the crowd, bringing you away and together, away and together. A man in an electric wheelchair divides the throng, and you wait stuck behind a lamppost. A little rush, and then another.

"What beautiful wooden flowers" Marge exclaims, pointing at a wooden posy in a wooden pot. The pot has slots in the top for stems so the flowers can be arranged in different ways, and a small cabinet alongside has a selection of further blooms, some of them missing from their cut-out compartments, so you can see only their empty silhouettes.

"Pity it's obviously incomplete."

"Yeah" Marge concedes, and you amble along.

Another toy of your grandfather's was a thaumatrope. He had

a number of them, but your favourite was of a bunch of flowers. A circular disc of laminated card, on one side was the question "What makes this bottle like the Goddess Flora?" in cursive above a picture of a slate-blue vase. The other side answered "Because it is crownd with flowers" below a bunch of faded, technicolour flowers. At the edges of the disc's meridian a string was attached to each side, by which lengths it could be held up. Twizzle the strings between thumb and forefingers and, in a rattling of card, it would spin and the flowers would be in the bottle, the question asked and answered, the bottle holding the flowers, the flowers the bottle of flowers in the bottle of flowers in the bottle the flowers in flowers the flowers. The bottle. The flowers.

To you this had never been an item of joy alone but was also one of despair. The sense of ambiguity, of proximity amidst undeniable separation, made you feel it was incumbent upon you, your duty, to spin and spin the disc so that the flowers were always in the vase, the terrible fact of their separation seeming something utterly alone. On one side: the flowers lost in a void. On the other: an empty vase.

With Margaret, at this point in your relationship, experiencing the silences between you gave forth an emotion like that, a sense of terrible ambiguity. Was this stunned silence or unspeakable delight? Was it no need to speak or no more to say? Is this ease, or abandonment of another kind—or is it between the two? Could it be not binary but both? At times Margaret began to seem a quantity entirely unknown, a stranger of whom it was impossible to have any knowledge at all, to garner any inkling of what she was thinking. Whether a silence was of delight or despair it seemed impossible to know until it was broken and the contents revealed.

"Did you see the birds?" you too-loudly ejaculate into the white.

"Yeah" she says, then "Hey, look at that guy's dungarees."

"Yeah." You pause, reflect. "What."

At one of the stalls there is a man in his late twenties with long brown hair, the ends of it died a kind of orangey blonde, browsing over a tray of silver spoons. He has a nose with a thickened bridge where it looks like it has been broken, but he wears it as though it were handsome. He is tall. He is wearing yellow dungarees. To you he looks Australian.

"What about them?"

"I just thought they looked cool" she muses breezily, defiantly. You move on.

The objects you pass look, some of them, as though they might be about to speak. A fender, all its fires burnt out. Wooden bric-a-brac blocks that would get chipped anew now only in transportation. Half a dozen tiny cups in sterling silver of too impractical a size and material for use, and which stand shining together in a huddle on the tablecloth, cold and glinting, blinking in the sunshine after upheaval from their home in a glass-fronted cupboard. No longer a part of a life, these objects take on an indeterminate expression, removed from their long-accustomed usage or undisturbed place and unable to decide if they are waste yet or not. Abstracted from their settings they have been grouped according to an unhomely rationale; unfamiliar teapots unused to the company of others their own size stand alongside each other awkward and plump. Old-style tennis rackets meet in a cardboard box, drawn together like ancients in an old-people's home by nothing more than an era in common, breaking dry cat-gut. An asthmatic dust rises from everything, a miasma of arborous decay under ink or acid, and the bitter bite of rust. Sheet music shedding papers in piles messy and unsorted. Dented, plastic-covered children's books that look grubby and contagious. Twenty-four volume illustrated encyclopaedias with cloth covers, one entry in the set prolifically marked in inscrutable handwriting (L – Lighthouse). A rotting and tarnished Louis XV wine rack priced at a fortune and which you wouldn't have accepted for free. A box of bicycle bells, their rings and springs rung together and jingling, shrill lives once limited to anger or joy. Whoopee or get out of the way. Brash shine or rust.

This is the boredom of things. They seem to ask: are we done with? Is it over? Their only message is clear: we are things with which others have become bored, sometimes to death. Are we to be restored?

You are both drawn in by a marquee selling lights. Although their individual puissance is somewhat diffused in the daylight, the effect of the fifty or a hundred lamps in the interior of the tent is a kind of white brightness of the air. There are table lamps with bronze women in figure-clinging dresses holding the bulb; a box with the words *Pepsi-Cola* in neon; floor lamps like searchlights or old-style spotlights from a movie set; a traffic light, slowly turning red, orange, green, orange, red, green, at a moronically even pace; the warning strobes of sirens affixed to upright wooden panels; one lamp in the shape of a giant, cream-coloured lightbulb; another a naked filament in an open, apparently real human skull.

It was the first time she had spoken enthusiastically all day.

"I had this friend who collected lights."

As soon as you hear it you find yourself waiting for a pronoun—wondering if he is male, and what kind of a friend.

"He had all things like this, Chinese lanterns, a dolls' house that gave bright light from all its windows, like, a big frontage sign, and a really gross one like that was a skull with a light in it. Like a bulb in it." Was she turned on by this? "His apartment was like something magic." She had been in his apartment?

"Oh wow" you emit automatically.

"Yeah, it was awesome." She is animated. She glances at you quickly, smiling. "Isn't it funny how lights change the atmosphere, and what we mean by that. Like how somewhere feels emotionally."

"Yeah, like the aura of a place." You manage to participate but you have become divided. Part of you knows that this is all reasonable, innocent, and ratchets out normal responses. But a switch has flicked and the other is concerned with this man, only this man, nothing else.

"Right" she continues. "Or different kinds of light. I guess it's partly a chemical change, with your hormones and your circadian rhythms changing, your ability to produce vitamin D and stuff like that, those must make a difference to how you feel. I mean, we know they do with like sunlight affective disorder or whatever."

Marge was liable to run on like this. There is a pause as you try to think about it, and struggle to suppress other thoughts.

"How did you know the guy, was he someone you knew from university?" You have tried already to head off the answer and to suggest you had a particular, different cast of thought in the asking—as though you might have been contemplating whether it was his university room decorated with the lights, the better to imagine it. But she said apartment. Well, he could have had an apartment.

She smiles and doesn't look at you. What the fuck does that mean? Is it pleasure at detecting your jealous ruse, or scorn at your fatiguing insecurity? Or didn't she hear you?

"He was Rachel's boyfriend, from just after we left."

There is a silence. Then you offer: "You're right though that it's not just what you said, because also tiny changes make a difference, like fairy lights which don't actually change the brightness of a room at all but make quite a change of atmosphere."

"Sure."

Is she hurt, now, at your oblique contradiction? Though you meant to conciliate. Or is she merely relaxed? Was this whole bit about the lights guy provocation or participation? Was it confession or simply confidence? Like the thaumatrope it is one, both, one, another, both.

The last marquee sells only wind chimes, some rusted, others bright. Shrill, they shiver in the wind and huddle closer for warmth but, knocking together, make only sound.

The silences, after this, began to thicken, to take on definite weight. You have subsequently wondered if it was by the very act of contemplating the collapse of the relationship that you broke it; whether you filled the silences with the very significance you dreaded they already had. But, however it happened, whereas previously the silences had flickered in ambiguity between ecstatic understanding and frigidity, now they take on a definite weight of reserve, of hard expansion by cold.

Although it is yet spring, now when you see her it is as though the frost blowing in between you is literal. Her limbs appear to have started to stiffen, are listless, arms left to swing pendulous by her sides or to lie slack on tabletops as though seized and slowed by cold. She appears, at moments, stunned by the chill into catatonic attitudes, mouth left long hanging open a touch, eyes dazed, as if about to wake with warmth to why she should leave you. As though her senses have been dulled she is slower to respond to your advances; you place a pacific hand on the small of her back and she does not react, seems from numbness not to feel it, until you rub and bring, by friction, warmth; then she turns to you with a slow smile, her features slowed as if by snow. No longer does she respond with hot (though thin) lips pecking at you like a delicate bird when you touch her, but a rigidity has set in. She is less viscous during sex, less loose and warm and wild of lip and limb, but angular now, and more jointed, and sensitive to sudden pain if you are clumsy, or made by her to feel so. She is not unwilling but not willing—the former would almost be, for showing some passion, preferred—and she shuts eyes and finds sleep soon after, face down in the pillows (don't disturb me!) as though entirely relaxed—but more than relaxed; gone. Or else she takes her absence somewhere else, leaping up after, suddenly lithe as though nothing had happened, to make a hot chocolate or send a work email she just really ought to finish right now quickly. You want to shake her awake, rouse her as with brandy or with blows, but your storm cannot penetrate the white.

In causality, now, the events and scenes are jumbled—their exact heredity you can't recall. It was all closely causal-seeming at the time, one thing leading inexorably to another, but now the events appear to you without order. Did you become distressed upon finding out that she had gone to the theatre with her male friend before or after she came to Shabbat dinner? And after Rebecca's birthday party, when you complained of being ignored and seated at the far end of the table, with that dullard John, and thus made a quarrel out of her enjoyable evening—was that before or after the Valentine's day steak, and sex on her flatmates' leather sofa since they were out? It all felt so reasoned at the time, so closely felt, as if your emotions had meaning and just cause; a clockwork sense of fact, one act presaging the next. But the greater abstraction of retrospect, the unapparence of order, shows something perhaps more true: the movement of the currents that ran beneath. There is, you reflect, perhaps an inevitability to interactions between people, to the outcomes of relationships, that has nothing to do with one thing leading to another, with anything that actually happens. Two personalities meeting are much less like ships exchanging semaphore on the surface than the tides which draw them together, which may rend them apart. Deep calls unto deep, and perhaps events are just the excuse of armature for what would happen anyway, of mutable and liquid significance and bent only by the wills of their actors to meanings thrust upon them.

Many things, indeed, seemed to have no consistent signification at all. Margaret's rather ringing, English voice; the way she picked through a salad as though she were turning over a flowerbed searchingly or were gardening; the two years she had spent in Florence, speaking Italian; the way cats seemed to come to her and she would stroke them absent-mindedly without looking at them: at the beginning these facts were enthralling, possessed of an almost magical quality. Why you cannot say, but later they became despite yourself unconscionably repugnant. You wanted to like them but ceased to be able to do so. At the start every thought of her tits titillated, even under clothes as she walked beside you, watery and quivering in her bra like cups of crème caramel. Later, this and the odd synonymy of their flatness with the mole on her cheek disturbed you; later still you lost any sense of it, forgetting her bodily beside you.

DOLL

Margaret wanted galleries and street art; you wanted vinyl sellers and music shops. To begin with you had each delighted in these interests of the other, hers made interesting to you simply because they were hers; they became, therefore, yours too, and vice versa. But that light tarnished, and you could no longer compromise. Once you had been enthralled by the insider knowledge which seemed to make ordinary street corners places of secret discovery. Now to stop to look at street art—framed A5 photographs of noses glued to walls around the South Bank, or vulgar (you thought) and sketchy miniature oil paintings of flowers affixed above the street names in Notting Hill—is insipid, insipidly trendy, and slowing. She's always staring around at it, not paying attention, when you have somewhere to go. And your music shops, you are sure, have gone for her from gilded cabinets under the beck of your knowledge and skill to reminders of her failed instrumentalism. She learned flute and piano as a child— 'like all of them', you can't stop yourself from adding mentally as sardonic addendum—but later let them, as well as her own painting, slide.

The details are shifting; the archetypes unchanged. The hurt of a loved one burning the part of themselves that loves you away is eternally the same. First they numb the tissue, keeping that area of themselves which has begun to reject you hidden, by tincture of guilt, from their own senses—then only from yours. Because it seems so unfair to you. Because they aren't yet sure of anything. Because they think you wouldn't understand—but you can tell there is an affliction. You smell it like a dog smells sickness. Next the malevolence grows—it never recedes once contracted—but until there is a full alteration you feel it only through absence, through realising that something is gone, that a thing between

148

you has slipped away without your notice—without any positive symptoms but merely a decline in condition. You scramble, then, desperately to find it; vex and pester the patient; are irritable—unreasonably, because you haven't been given a reason, because of the change which she denies is happening—and she retains the prerogative of the infirm: I'm just not feeling well, that's all. You must leave her alone. It's an effort, but you manage it; you treat her with sudden, lavish kindness and care. Nothing changes. You relapse to anger as suddenly as you had reformed, demand her love as before, become a hypocrite, appear inconsiderate and inconstant, even feel so yourself. You do not have the eloquence or frankness of abjection to put words to what you intuit; that, in love, one is never too unwell to look loving on one's lover. In any case, you should not have to say it. But without the right words you make appeal only pulingly. Then you are needy, and asking too much; you even register and resent the sight of this in yourself but cannot hold back. How the anaemic or wilfully blind don't ask at all but persist in this rejected state for years you will never know, though you've seen it often enough. And she withdraws further, armed with excuse now by your angry fragility, and the further she withdraws the more grotesquely you clutch after her until, broken, sent out of reason by the undisclosed, unexplained disappearance of love, you go to the opening of the lithograph fair she has coordinated on New Bond Street and appear in tears. When you try to appeal to her and have her, simply with love, attend to you, you are hushed by her with fear in her eyes and of course this is too much, this is important to her, this was her one important day and she's been anxiously working desperately towards it for weeks and not everything is about you and she has a job to do which goes on regardless and you don't have perspective and you are making a scene.

There are, for you, no easy determinisms. Everything, at last, that was a necessary condition was therefore sufficient, because that past has flowed one way alone: to this. It was the lump of sugar in your coffee one frosty morning months ago as much as it was her frosting over over over two or three months. Was it walking next the rusty merry-go-round, or was it amidst the porcelain coffee cups as evening sang its song to dusk? Was the top set spinning by a childish kiss in the playground, many years ago, or was the moment of last choice and no return much later? Have you been moving or been moved? And, having been, was it always to be? If it happened thus, was it always thus to happen? Could the signs be made to mean something different? Were you always to have parted, thus?

We see, it seems, causality from our point of disadvantage in the middest—the lightswitch believing that it caused the light. From thence there are the shadows and semblances, the sensible, sensical gravities of meaning and motive, of echo and response. Only if you could also see with the perspective of the wooden bench, the stars, the lump of sugar and the milk falling apart in your coffee would all dissolve itself in world, and you would know. In world, and not in cause, that is: for that paradoxical idea carries within itself the notion of no-cause, an imaginary opposite which reveals the impossibility of both. There is only one side to this coin. If you could be in everything, even the inanimate, you would see it all. Were you always to have parted, thus?

And so, at the last, you find yourself seated in a cast iron chair on the terrace of Fulham Palace, opposite Miss Margaret Howard and Mrs Cece Howard, her mother, and overlooking a large expanse of lawn. Only two or three other tables are taken, all at sufficient distance from you and sufficiently hushed by the thick dusky air and the sense of quiet solemnity it draws down upon its subjects that you are undisturbed and uninhibited; free to play at palaces. At the closest of these tables two women, sisters, surely, communicate in sign language between long intervals spent staring into the gathering summer air. Other parts of the Palace are older, but this side presents the face of a Georgian manor house; a long reach of flat façade punctuated by white French windows which lead from the Drawing Room Café to the terrace where you now take tea. Tucked around one corner of the building is an adjoining chapel, a sombre and dark Victorian addition, its windows a purple that looked almost black as you approached in the fading light, and in front of you, across the immaculate lawn ending with a short sweep of roughage and weeds, is the red brick of the Tudor walled garden, a small black gate cut into it.

"It's called Bishops' Park" Mrs Howard had told you on your way through the grounds "because this used to be the seat of the Bishop of London. That walled garden is planted in flowers that grow in the colours of the coat of arms of one of them: red, blue and yellow. Oh it's just absolutely my favourite place in this city, I make sure to come every time I visit."

Mrs Howard's voice is a vision of Margaret's to be; it has crackled with age, a kind of vocal fry of alcohol's dotage, dry whites and dry crackers, desiccation in starched shirt collars— dry-cleaned then wrapped in loose bags of filmy plastic—and afternoons on the porch, where she conspires with her singular friend (of circumstance, proximity and consumption) to hide their drinking from themselves. An eminently social deceit, each plays the role of persuading the other against her better judgement so both have excuse to offer to conscience later; the next day; ever. From what you have been told Margaret's parents aren't very happily married. Probably why the father isn't also in town.

You watch a squirrel descend a tree across the lawn. After meeting at the main gates you had strolled through the park, all three, in a daze of mottled sunlight beneath which stepped Cece and Margaret's two terrifying pairs of flats, cracking seed cases and crushing nettles underfoot—you are sure that both these women drink them in their tea, stings and all. Mrs Howard has flown over to visit for a week and to see Marge's fair. She lives in Hong Kong where, you imagine, she conducts a ladies-who-lunch lifestyle, playing the fashionable empire ex-pat in a manner hard to sustain, nowadays, anywhere else. But she runs, Marge told you, a private fashion salon; buying clothes from small designers she sells them to her friends at séances in her front room, and has come to London via Paris.

Cece is a small sharp woman not without expressions of kindness, but who appears both nervy and finely controlled. Her face might once have been pretty, and a more handsome nose than her small one could almost have granted it something more; her full hair is cut in a smart bob, and has turned a kind of cupreous silver where, you know from a photograph of Margaret's, it once rivalled the lustre of a seal brown mare. Her eyes have unfortunate circles beneath them, and she is wearing a stylish coat with blocky panels and a cutaway at the neck in dark, imperial green with decorative gold buttons. Mrs Howard wears her height as though to be any bigger is something somewhat shameful, but her daughter, when strolling alongside, is a taller and more lissom mistress. Today Marge is wearing a white silk blouse with ties knotted at the neck, in rather your idea of a 50s air hostess, and is carrying a thin leather jacket. You are already sure when you meet that she's later going complain of cold. She is not looking at you too often, and her comportment is unreadable except for what you so far make out as a placid determination to 'get on'. You are left, still, even now, with the feel of the paint chipping and crisped on black metal railings, ailing, and on their gates as you hold them open on your way through the park. Warm from the sun, this coating coming off and sticking to your palms so you have to brush it off quite thoroughly. The dry earth that is turning to but not yet arrived at dust, at dusk. It does not rise in clouds or choke but it is, yet, light and warm enough to scent the air. As you watch, the squirrel cascades down the tree and along the lawn like held fermata. Note held into leap, the tail following. Note held into leap.

"Pass the butter, would you darling?" Mrs Howard calls to you across the table, scone at the ready. You shimmy into action. It is never the time to end things.

You were supposed to think about it. You were supposed to think about it. You and Margaret had met the night before to discuss what to do. Things weren't working between you. To be frank. Was there something to be done. You had decided both to sleep on it and to think it over this morning, her at her Saturday job in the gallery and you at home, practising, preparing, whatever constituted the duties you pretended you needed to perform to avoid the shame of bringing another 'nothing' to drop at her feet at close of day when she asked you what you had been doing. And yet you despised the disdain for your inactivity which you read into those silences, knowing that this nothing was important somehow. You had parted quietly that night, both delivering 'I-love-you' like a concession to saddening truth. Was it to be fixed.

And then, when you meet, it is as though nothing has happened.

In the middle of the next morning, while you were dawdling, Margaret had written to invite you to meet her mother for tea. After your fiasco at the opening of the lithograph fair four days earlier any previous intimation of a meeting between you and Margaret's family had been waylaid. But mother was leaving the next day, so this was the only chance; M's hand was forced. Had Marge really been contemplating that she might not introduce you? Although you could countenance that you might be about to end your relationship, all the same this appeared to you an act of special brutality. Her mother came over so rarely, and she and Marge communicated so often. Marge had even been to yours for Shabbat dinner, for Christ's sake. Was she so ashamed of you? Even now that she had invited you it felt patronising, as if Margaret were granting you this interview as a last chance. Possibly it was just that—an interview. Perhaps this was the final test of mettle, a second opinion on your worth.

When you arrived at the gates and walked up to meet them you found them talking, it seemed, of sunglasses. Conversation, during the twenty minutes' walk through the park to the palace café, had been light, and Margaret and her mother clearly thought it more apposite to chatter on small private subjects—Bob had got his motorboat licence, you discover—than to lapse into silence, which very fact suggested that Cece might be in full command of the state of things between you and M. Or was she? It could be that this was Margaret's ruse alone and Mrs Howard was less canny than she looked. Her talk was awkwardly abridged by crowbar comments asking you about your life and music, which Cece seemed, in sudden flurries, energised to assay then suddenly exhausted of capacity to pursue, as if the answers you began upon sustained so little interest or were uttered in so foreign a language that she abandoned enquiry altogether.

And now you are here, taking tea. Around the lawn are large, venerable trees of grave but benignant demeanour; a copper beech shimmering, a sycamore letting spinners drop like jokes. Not two hundred feet away to the right, beyond the trees, invisible and inaudible, runs the Thames. It is just this inaudibility which lets you know that it is there, the lacuna of large silence scalloped out of London streets. Here and in other parts of the palace evening sings of: the descent of light, the return of birds to their nesting places, crannies and nooks in branches, the last glint of sunlight on the silver-edged tea service out on the terrace before it becomes dun, the unfurling of the time for furtive whispers, the time at which first kisses can be sprung by the garden onto couples, the gradual then suddenly complete disappearance of colours, the clattering of things in high-beamed kitchens somewhere in readiness for supper, the whooshing sound of swinging doors, the whooshes getting shorter and coming in quicker succession until the door just wobbles in the frame, the scraping of birds barely visible against sky, the final darkness that comes upon water. Last, ringing in your ears, the fading out of bells from the church nearby, All Saints, that you only hear after they have sounded—only realise were sounding in silence. Were they truly ringing?

Their ringing in your ears and the sudden lull that ensues breaks your silent reflection, an internal tumult about the situation that results in external paralysis. You catch a glimpse of yourself as others must, you 'remember where you are', and, like the exhausted or the very drunk, find that you don't know how long you've been dazed in contemplation as mother and daughter talk—perhaps a minute, perhaps ten—or whether it has been noticeable. You had been absently contemplating the side of Margaret's face. She must have noticed. You have no idea what they have been talking of, or how long ago, but you find yourself asking, in panic and at random, "How was the weather while you were in Paris?"

"Oh it was ghastly most of the time. I had to hole up in the Louvre, but I got out a bit more on Thursday when it was a little brighter."

"The Parisians don't like the rain" you proffer.

"No one does. Do you like the rain?"

This throws you into confusion, because you don't want to say you do and to contradict Mrs Howard completely, and nor therefore to be thought deliberately to court eccentricity or to be wilfully perverse. But nevertheless you really do feel a certain kinship with the rain, which gets a bad rap. You think one should like all weathers.

"I don't mind the rain" is all you muster. For want of a smarter rebuff you turn down to your tea, looking markedly away to cut the slice of cake you haven't been eating for the last ten minutes. She isn't paying attention.

Perhaps few people like the rain...but some dislike it more than others, and the French are like cats; they do disappear when it pours. When it rains in London there are still people flooding into the streets. In Paris? Nothing. That has been true whenever you've been there, anyway. All taxis instantly clicked into *occupé*, no sorties made to take drinks. You continue this internal argument, rankling into your cake as you cut it exactingly into smaller, more regimented slices. 'I'm a man for all seasons.' That would have been a good response. No good now. *Trepverter* was what your grandmother used to call such imaginary ripostes. Stair-words.

"They're so peculiar, the Parisians" she is going on. "Very cultured but very peculiar. They abhor violence but have no moral qualms when it comes to sex—there were bare-chested women in adverts, on bus stops or the little news kiosks, displaying themselves in lingerie or what have you. Just everywhere. They're so shocking and so easily shocked."

"You know, there's something that seems kind of natural in that" you aver. "It seems kind of sweet to me. Like, not everybody has a gun but everybody, really, is naked under their clothes."

"Darling, speak for yourself!" crackles Cece, dramatically bridling.

You have to laugh, and Margaret emits a shrill peal. "Mother!" she exclaims, as you wish you'd made a joke as good.

What was said next you can't recall, because Margaret's flirtatious amusement at her mother's joke strikes you dumb and still, returning you to private reflection. Why this should be you can't quite make out at first, but gradually you feel rather than think your way to the certain impression that Marge's social ease and levity is appalling, given the context. How can she laugh, when things are teetering so between you? Either this is something strangely heartless, or it shows a capacity for dissimulation you had not seen before, or both. Or perhaps, it dawns on you, as you are running now with great and sudden strides of repressed feeling, is it not just cold but vicious, her gaiety a pitiless taunt to show up your dumb gravity? Can it be?

For what seems like an age the tea has been standing on the table. The desultory talk, interspersed with what seem to you to be long periods staring out at the dusk and the sky, works on you maddeningly. You have skipped out some introductory phase in the relationship with Mrs Howard, and by extension in today's meeting with Margaret, and gone straight to a state of jaded comfort. Possibly, after all, Marge's behaviour isn't coldness but cover for some blind fault of yours for which she is trying to make up in front of her mother. You are flooded with the feeling that there is something you should have said, some protocol that has been horrifically lacking, and this brings silent, mounting desperation. The suspense is unbearable. You can't sit in silence for much longer. What is it they expect from you?

All at once it occurs to you that the teapot has been sitting there for the longest time, and that neither Marge nor her mother has touched it. Holy fuck, they must be waiting for you to pour. You don't know what rules Marge expects to be in force when her mother is around, and the recent distance combined with the suddenness of the invitation haven't given you the chance to get either coached or calmed. Mrs Howard, perhaps, has exotic manners, those prized by an English ex-pat living in Hong Kong, a carefully guarded cultural artefact that blossoms weirdly and wildly in that open climate, becomes a baroque show-flower cultivated into extra blooms and flourishes. Plus she's older; haven't you read somewhere of the men pouring at tea? They must both have been just waiting for you, and you sitting here oblivious—

"Oh my God, please let me—"

"Oh, wait a minute there darling, it has yet to brew" Mrs Howard says calmly.

Margaret looks at you with an embarrassed smile, the meaning of which must be either shame at your dullness or scorn. You had naturally assumed, from her apparent cool determination to 'get on', that you had been suffering through this together, that for her as for you there was the sense of something suspended, the sensation of something on hold that you were both desperate, really, to drop character and talk about, but you realise now that this may not be the case at all. It is replaced by the flash of thought, persuasive almost by virtue of its perversity, that Margaret has brought her mother as a shield—precisely in order that she does not have to talk to you. Is she so ingenious? Many minutes pass in contemplation of this new horror as of a new vista suddenly torn open in the sky of a familiar view. When you next look about you the sign language sisters have left. Mrs Howard lifts up the lid of the teapot circumspectly, peering in, and then with a judicious air removes, with a spoon, one teabag from inside. As she deposits it on the side of her saucer it quinces its mouth and sniggers, crumpling up its face, astringent and wry.

She sends the teapot to confess to your cup, spilling its guts briskly and resolutely as you imagine Cece herself might make confession, and then returns it to brew silently in the middle of the table. In her firmness not a drop is spilt, but for you the spouts of jugs bespeak a promise always betrayed, and as you add milk to your tea some, of necessity, runs down the sides of the little porcelain jug and drips to fill your saucer. You sink with the spillage, wallowing in the dish but similarly unable to diffuse through the enamel and disappear. Your spoon reflects, taking a moment to think about the scene, taking in the scene to think about the moment. It is taking in and turning over everything as you pick it up, making caricatures of you and the evening light, and you hide its ironic face quickly in the tea, blurring the milk to bits in expiation.

"Oh, Rebecca's dog came back" Margaret announces, irrelevantly.

"What?" you respond.

The knife says something cutting to the cake, which splits its sides in laughing and goes all to pieces.

"Yes. Mummy I told you when it ran off on a walk on the heath. Well, almost a week later she came back from work and he was curled up on the doorstep of her apartment, much much thinner and all covered in earth but basically fine."

"No!" says Mrs Howard, shocked.

"Yeah! They think he probably crawled down a rabbit hole, chasing a rabbit, and got stuck, and then could only get out when he got thin enough to move."

"Oh how wonderful that he found his way home all safe. Poor little dear thing!"

"I know, isn't that crazy J?"

"Gosh I know" you say as enthusiastically as you can muster, but it feels inadequate. You are a drowning man.

What was the significance of this story? Was there a reason she was telling it to you now? You look into her unreadable eyes for an answer. Both women, it seems to you, are politely ignoring what must appear as your bizarre manner in the way they might ignore a bad smell, exchanging knowledge of it only through glances when you aren't looking.

You can't make Margaret out at all. You cannot gauge Margaret, at all. She seems irretrievably distant, her significance shifting in a heat haze. Why has she brought you here? Your psyche makes some far off hedonic calculation; it will cost too much to discover if she is playing you or not; whether she wants you or is trying to get rid of you, to find it out will exact too much pain. If she is merely dandling you from her fingertips you know it will break you; if she is not you don't know how you are supposed to find it out, left alone as you are, without her warmth. As you are making this intuitive calculation Mrs Howard rises and steps inside to look for more sugar, and you are left, for the first time, with Margaret and horribly alone. You turn to look at her, and she responds with a complacent smile, a smile overmuch absent from her eyes, and then turns to the landscape, leaving you with the side of her face to look at in a manner which deliberately makes it awkward for you to continue to keep your head ostentatiously turned to stare in her direction. You must act now or be doomed: you must, in this second, make a decision as to this woman.

"Margaret" you call to her, still looking at her face, an appeal to her heart. She turns to you that bland, artfully meaningless smile. This was meant to be the moment to break the social façade and squeeze hands, smile lovingly, whisper 'I love you', but her airy attention brooks no opportunity. You falter a moment—but you cannot fail yourself now.

"I simply can't see you under these conditions."

She does not move in the slightest, is unnaturally still, but it is as though she is seizing, petrifying, a hardening tension beneath the skin tightening her together. If she is feigning shock only because she wants you to continue, to compel you to carry this out and not risk saying anything that might stop you, her performance is immaculate. At this moment Mrs Howard steps out towards you from the French windows. You stand up.

"Thank you for this afternoon, Miss Howard" you say to her gravely as she approaches. To her credit she doesn't break her stride, but merely widens her eyes and raises her eyebrows at you in detached surprise, then turns to look at Margaret for information as she nears the table. You turn away.

For a single, grand, triumphant moment you are sailing away from the table and onto the grass. You are moving in perfect grace, grandeur and comportment. A tricky business, no doubt about it, but sometimes a brusque end has to be brought to such things.

You weren't to be taken advantage of like that; it's your life after all. But wait. Miss Howard. You called Margaret's mother *Miss* Howard. You can feel their eyes at your back as you start to walk away across the lawn in the darkening evening and the light starts to fall out of your deed. What you have embarked upon darkens as it becomes clear to you. It is an immensely long lawn, you begin to realise, and you must now walk alone across the entire span of it under observation, right in the middle of the grass. The direction in which you have assailed it was chosen simply because it presented an open field away from the manor house and its guests, but without consideration as to where you were heading. What you find now is that you have struck off across the middle of a vast, empty field, pointed in roughly the direction of the little black gate in the side of the Tudor walled garden. It is perhaps forty metres away. You cannot turn back. They must be looking at you. You attempt to look noble but not proud, to affect in your walk a gait of sufficient solemnity for the moment, but also of normality, to pass off this utterly final, bizarre, incontrovertible thing you have done as within the bounds of normalcy, simply by your ease, but it is of course impossible. Absurd. A man leaving his lover and her mother and striding away across the lawn for minutes, whole minutes spent disappearing dramatically into the evening. Your grave announcement. 'I simply can't see you under these conditions.' What was that?

You have, nevertheless, managed to make it about halfway along the lawn before your gait begins to collapse. Perceiving how you must be perceived it is as if the keys of their gazes turn cogs in your joints, behind your knees and inside your ankles, loosen you at the hips, play a rhythm upon your stops that phase-shifts against your normal metronome of pace, and you begin to feel like a puppet jangling away across the grass. You can only hope to affect any kind of normality now, as you start swinging your arms in a way you first imagine will be a natural manner but which immediately feels like anything but, feels like a toy soldier or a self-satisfied banker in a black and white film, a maniac levity after such an absurd display. Of course you can't stop it suddenly now either. Surely they are talking about you. Is Margaret weeping into her cup? Or are they both just watching you sail away in silence, seated and sipping their tea? You can't hear anything from behind you. "What a *bizarre* person" perhaps she's saying. "Well, darling, if you ask me it's obviously for the best. Gosh, what a nasty ending he made of it, but doesn't that just *prove* it's the right decision. Thank goodness he did, *I* say!" Oh Jesus Christ. Your legs are weakening. You're going to fall down in a moment. "And isn't he Jewish anyway?"

Oh fuck. Oh Jesus fuck. You'd forgotten to pay. You'd just walked away, not even offering. That's rude by any definition. Will they notice, amidst all the shock? Your knees are shaking now like those of a newborn fawn. They're right to want to be rid of you. They are bound to notice you didn't even offer any contribution when they get up to leave. Your face is a mask of anguish; it feels like a blank on your body since it is the only part they cannot see, and which you do not have to control for view. To try to take your own attention away from your malfunctioning legs you squeeze your features into a wince of self-disgust and pain, and close your eyes, and your legs are about to give way, you can't feel them anymore, and you're just there in front of the little gate to the garden, and you push on it just as you start to stumble, and your knees buckle, and you completely collapse, surrounded by dahlias in red and blue and yellow, as the last strains of trumpet blow out, and you slip backwards, all the way back, into Solomon's black leather chair. Applause. And then the moving coil pickup on the vinyl, Mono CL 2306 *My Funny Valentine*, hits dead wax, with a skipping thud, static.

"So. What did you think?" says Solomon who, in an unexpected wisdom of tact for which you are grateful, had somehow noted and managed to partake of your silence, listening to the whole fifteen minute record there with you in his strange office.

"Wonderful" you tell him. "It's the best quality pick-up I've ever heard."

The rest of the day passes easily; the simple act of contemplation in listening to old memories has brought you to a kind of settled peace. You come home tired and wistful but basically happy. It had been a long, long day, and you'd done about as much emotional processing—not to mention musical work—as you can handle. In looking back on all that stuff with Marge you'd managed to achieve a kind nostalgia, a forgiving euphoria of retrospect which you feel proud to have attained. Nevertheless now, after a tiring but satisfactory day, you have nothing left, content to remain pleasantly stunned by the sheer busyness and complexity of it all into a kind of detachment. The world is far away and you are set back from it, like a medallion in a museum case nestled in foam or a book in its place at the back of a shelf. You take the Underground home in this cloud of yourself. Sure, the music today wasn't totally satisfying—laying down music that is by nature improvised seldom is, and one is always taunted by the idea that if you could do just one more take it might come out perfect. But experience tells you that listening a few days later will obliterate your consciousness of the flaws and show up the track much better than you had remembered it, when you aren't so focussed on what you could have done. You breathe out in relaxation as you step through the door of your apartment, and press the button flashing on your home phone.

"Hello?"

It's your own voice.

"Hello darling, are you there? Can you hear me?"

What?

"Hello! Hey, how are you?"

Shit.

"Yeah it's good thanks. Been recording with some of the guys at the studio this morning, which has been going pretty well. We laid down some good takes this morning and I'm just on break now."

You suppose you still are. You drop your saxophone case limply to the carpet.

"Yeah. I just thought I'd skip out to say hello and see how you were doing."

You sit down in the middle of the floor in the hallway.

"What kind of thing?"

You look at her, visible through the door to your bedroom, sitting on a chair.

"Mmm, something funny? Or something with action?"

Huh.

"Ok, let me think about it and I'll send you some ideas later."

You look at the little red light on the phone blinking.

"Well how do you feel?"

You lie back on the carpet, tears prickling behind your eyes. You rub your knuckles into them, and when you open them your voice asks "What! What is it?"

"No. You're a darling. But you must tell me. What is it."

You look up at the ceiling.

"Urh. Dammit. Well, I can't wait. I'll try to come home early. Ok. I love you."

Fuck.

Soon, then, you start to want her constantly, terribly, even beyond your capacity to effect anything. Your orgasms don't satiate as much as aggravate, like scratching a sore; they're just wishes dropped in a well, never filling it, never bringing up water. Is it common to be thirsty after you come? You are. First just occasionally, then almost always, and unquenchably so. Lying next to her after rolling out as your soft fluid pools or slides inside her, the hair on the front of your body where it pressed against her matted by sweat, holding her hand or wrist or forearm barely more thick, you're overcome by thirst. Not even for water but just by pure desire—thirst being a sensation so close to pure need that it's how this want manifests to your experience. But you never drink. It's the sort of desire that is so overpowering it prevents action.

Proportions, not people, set off this lust. You walk down the street and become aware, across the road and walking in tandem with you, of a female figure. It's not even, yet, really any picture of a person, just a set of anatomical measurements and visual cues that turn you on; the particular expression of legs pointed down to strappy beige leather heels; the thin poise of the ankle and its contrast with the thick side of the thigh, its muscular indentations twitching in and out of view through the slit of the fabric as the bulge of rounded quad pushes up the front of the pencil skirt, and already you know the expression of the squashed toes and their red nail varnish, the inexplicable attractiveness of the thicker pad of the big toe and the slightly roughened, outdoor skin of the foot in general. You recognise all this in your peripheral vision as an animal expert would recognise a giraffe amidst trees or tell a species. Occasionally you're misled, and when you hurry on so you can turn to look back and get a view of her face she's a woman much older, not attractive at all, and there's a sudden, nightmarish twist in reality. But usually, even if you discover something sordid or imperfect about her—the bulge or rolls of a stomach, on this particular woman, pushing out her top and slipping above the waistband of her skirt—it doesn't matter, you like her more for the imperfections, the dirty truths. She's less demanding and easier to desire, less impossible. You see a woman like this and, without thinking, your thought stops, and there is very little left of you except a pit of lust, and you must go home and fuck your doll. Quickly and roughly.

Looking absently out of your window you see that a woman walks the street below. Thinking herself unseen she licks the side of her mouth, to ease dry skin there, or because of rain she wants to taste, or because there is a sweet almond smear from a tuile just eaten, or merely to stretch out her tongue, just to feel its strength. But you see this and eat her with your eyes until she is out of sight, yank the drapes closed hurriedly, rushing, and go to shove your dick in your doll's mouth, using it to blow out her cheek from inside and then rubbing it across her lips and patting it over her eyes. This woman's private moment, the unabashed tongue, its ambiguity, the fact that she has revealed herself privately for you as to a voyeur god; this makes you wild. Wild in part because she didn't know you were watching, because you'd never unlock that sluttish tongue from a beautiful woman, because she would never stretch out to lick you with such abandon as that sugary smear on the side of her mouth.

But, more often than things outside the flat, your doll inside starts to turn you on. All sexual paths end in her. It's a desire worse than pain that teases you until you feel spun out to a filament, pulled to just a fine thin line. It's the constant sight of her that is most unremitting, and after a while anything sets you off. Her foot out from under the blanket—even if she's totally covered up—even if you've covered her up—the tempting nonchalance of that cocked, pale heel. The sudden globular arc of a tit, even if veiled by the duvet—sometimes especially then, since it's there to be discovered, to have your memory of what it looks like meet reality again. Is that why we fuck—remembering? Because our memories are inadequate to turn us on? And then the hair, cheap, painfully clean platinum blonde hair to be grabbed in fistfuls, to run your hand through, to brush across your face. What satisfaction is to be found there? It's not in pure touch, nor merely sensual gratification. The hair on a male doll would repulse you. Here your desire is the only thing that does.

Made self-regarding by desire you soon begin to become conscious of her presence in a different way; you begin to choke. Whereas before you had walked taller, moved with greater purpose, been inspired to new heights on the saxophone by sensing her there, her as a part of you—now, possibly from wanting her, she has become separate and you feel her too little; her gaze overmuch. When she sits where you have left her, upon the wooden chair facing out to the window, and although you deliberately refrain from looking in her direction, you know she sees you reflected in the window pane pressed against the black night, the light from inside showing you up. Even with eyes averted from her gaze you feel it heavily. Whereas before you might have gone striding through the sitting room, now when you try to do so something is out of place. You can see that you are walking, and you are making a satisfactory progression from one end of the room to the other—first because you wanted to get to the kitchen, now merely to practise your own pacing—but something is awry. Under her gaze, as under the purview of an attractive woman you notice walking behind you in the street, you seem to forget how to walk.

You balance; you lift one leg before the other; you progress across the carpet; perhaps it is invisible that you are not walking aright, but you know that you are not. Your paces do not fill the spaces they should—they are too long, or too short. Your timing is off—too hurriedly quick, or too deliberately slow. You don't swing your legs as you ought—you lift them at the hip, rather than swinging them forward like pendulums, or perhaps you swing them too much and lift them too little. You seem to press each foot down into the ground where it should naturally fall into position. What was one motion—walking—is now six or seven, the scale staggered until it is no longer a glissando with each note sliding into the next, but a jagged fumble. With each misplaced pace your legs start to feel weaker. You try again, fail harder, feel her gaze more strongly, your embarrassment grows. What must she think, now, of you pacing erratically across the room in this way behind her? But you must prove that you can manage it, you must do one accomplished walk. There, that felt nearly right, but still there is something missing. Again.

Soon you begin to feel naked in front of her. The sensation of nudity is particular, and the beautiful, you are certain, forget their own shame. You, ashamed of your body, its pallor and hair and slightly stringy, hunched aspect and your small thick penis—you had felt the sensation of nudity, perhaps, longer than most. It starts for most people in the great nudity interregnum: betwixt childhood and sexual awakening. There's a period between the age of about ten, until which you're relatively unabashed, and later, when you take your clothes off for the first time in front of a partner, where your nudity becomes guarded. Then that first time undressing feels so much more naked than it does later on, when you're used to sex and have done it enough to not mind it or even think about the drill. But now, apparently, the sensation has made a late return, and you feel yourself colder and in the third-person.

Where you walk imperfectly, move imperfectly, appear in imperfect nudity, she is perfect in form and moving. She doesn't walk or move according to her own will, it's true, but it's because of this that each of her gestures is of a kind of ideal economy and grace. There is no affectation in her movement, since she never moves without cause. And in her nudity, which is not nudity because there is no consciousness of it being anything than as it should be, her perfect form is also a mockery of yours. She appears barely to weigh upon the sofa, barely to crease the covers. Everything *you* touch you sag and crumple; the more you try to pose to hide your imperfections—crossing naked legs to hide bulging bobbing penis, placing forearm over fold of stomach and covering belly discolouration—the more they feel made obvious, highlighted by the indiscretion of trying to be discreet. Curled about yourself you are a homunculus against her, the natural heft of her limbs—no more, no less—splaying her spread-eagled on the bed. And thus she does not disturb the universe.

One day you realise that she hasn't chosen you as you chose her. When she felt a part of you it wasn't even a question, but now you begin to wonder, since she's never been with another man, whether she prefers you at all. Does she really like you? She hasn't slept with anyone else, so how would she even know?

You begin to be tormented by sick fantasies. You become expert at finding ways in which you might have lacked precedence. In one particularly persistent fixation you envisage her in the workshop after they had finished making her, tied up in her box, mint condition and ready to be sent out to you, and one of the men, the man meant to seal her up, supposed to be professional and entrusted with that, is left alone and does something to her. Not even something terrifically sexual; he touches her vagina with a single finger, running down that infinitesimally corrugated mound on the outside, trailing her ever so lightly. Or if he doesn't even touch her he whispers "I love you" into her ear. He whispers this into the ear of every doll that comes through his hands, the sick fuck, to assert his precedence. To be the first man ever to have spoken to them in that way, to have whispered in that ear which another, some poor schmuck, would think they were the only man to woo. No doubt the workers joked and addressed the dolls jocularly on the factory floor, but you don't mind about that; as long as they were all there, and it was impersonal. No doubt they gave the dolls pet names, pretended they could use their tits to dim the lights or tune the radio, spoke into their breasts like intercoms. Or, at least, no doubt they did this when they first started on the job, before they became desensitised to it and the dolls stopped being funny, or until there came a severe foreman who disliked such horsing around, took the dolls very seriously, had some weirdly tyrannical possessiveness of them himself or simply an overactive conscience. The idea of games like that you didn't mind. It was this packing guy, the guy whispering into your doll's ear or even just looking at her with a lascivious thought, and it made you feel sick and sent a tightening pain down your spine.

After this—in accordance with it—her character seemed to

change. Whereas before you'd loved and felt eternally wanted by her open, spreading pussy, now it takes on a different expression. It looks no longer desirous and dedicated but gaping, prolific and wanton. It is more independent of you, as is she; her legs more frequently closed in rest, deliberately to provoke you to spread them; suddenly and paradoxically more open, too, to mock you with that indecent maw; and then her head falling from side to side as you fuck her in missionary, refusing to remain looking up and in a position to meet your eyes. She becomes enswathed with these fantasies of yours which you know are pernicious but which you cannot dismiss or manage to disperse; they are a quicksand that only constricts more tightly the more you thrash against it.

You start to hate your constant need for her. It's so inhuman. It's the dullard dog who gets uncontrollably turned on, a bitch messily bleeding profusely sloppily on the floor, or the cur pumping furniture and nearby knees like a maniac, composure lost and intelligence suddenly void and its horrific tongue wagging as it fucks. One of your childhood friends, Jamie, had a great big golden retriever, and you all used to play the game of crouching on the floor until it tried to mount and hump you. Fucking weird. You see its dumb blank face before you; the only expression on it apart from enthusiasm a look of surprise at its own actions with eyes pleading for explanation, a question rumpling the brows above as the tongue wags lax and licentious below, jaws in a parody of open-mouthed smile.

You know it's reasonless to be ground into such mercy. You hate her for it, and hate the women on the street for it, and hate yourself for hating them. After you're spent, having fucked her, and you find your naked face and body leaning above hers, still suspended now after that insanity of action, you can't countenance it. Having loved her in all the concupiscence of your desire your thought spins and spits back into your face and hers your grotesque lust, and you detest her. Having embodied what appeared to be a marvellous, supremely powerful desire—divine in its totality of purpose, its weight of importance and meaning—now she means nothing. This is the fall of all men: to see the things they love come arbitrary.

If you take this thought further, which you can hardly bear to do, you see all humanity and its creation as a kind of lewd masturbation over filth; the classical statues enshrining the proportions of the beautiful, Michelangelo's David, the Venus di Milo, all mistaken, wasting time on a form we believe god-given because we've relegated divinity to the pulse of our hormones from two hairy, papery sacs of testicles and a thick cock.

The saxophone too, that object to which you have devoted your life—how arbitrary and ridiculous it can suddenly seem. From a thing of grace and beauty—your chosen instrument—to a thing nonsensical and bizarre. Because you first saw one as a child you accepted its weirdness, but occasionally you come to see it with what feels like universal objectivity. Then you seem to perceive that there's nothing perfect or Platonic about its form; that it can be no absolute. Invented by an eccentric Belgian who started creating instruments at fifteen and named them all after himself, this was the only one that succeeded. And look at it. It's all buttons and tubes, hooks and curves and great fat lily-pad keys, odd factory-like valves and outputs opening and closing. You don't sit at it like a piano or hold it like a flute, you have to strap it around your neck and support it oddly by a hard sharp hook over your right thumb. Shake spit out of it when it fills up. Put little pieces of Rizla in your mouth for padding when you get sores on your gums. The muscles of your mouth and neck spasm from the odd contortions they have to achieve. The keys get stiff and stick down as saliva oozes through and have to be fixed by sliding paper shaded with graphite pencil underneath. It's wildly temperamental—can't be too hot, nor too cold, and the reeds crack and splinter suddenly and have to be replaced, soaked overnight before they can be used. Any movement you make changes the sound, any slight alteration of breath or posture. Sometimes it's as if it's affixed to your soul, stuck in to transmit your lungs. But then, at times of, perhaps, even greater clarity, you come to love it not in spite of but because of this absurdity. This must be that mature kind of love which accepts the beloved in all its lack of grace, wears no scales on its eyes, and loves the very weirdness of its object. It occurs to you that this is the best kind of love to have with people too, if you can manage it. You are not sure whether you have often or ever been able to do so.

You can't get to that place in love with the doll. At one moment you're mad about her and in a rage with beauty; at the next she's meaningless, and it makes as much sense to want her as it would to want any configuration of form—a tree or a triangle—and all women fall with her, their shapes losing any sense as symbols. You can't go on like this. Something must be done.

A sudden inspiration comes to you one morning, with the irrefutable force of the almost magical urge. You'll bring the doll out when Terry and Dave arrive. You are delighted at the idea of their surprise—you'll shock Terry for once, really knock him off his feet—and, made suddenly giddy in your excitement, you cannot think that there might be any downsides to this plan. The only negative possibility that occurs to you is that Terry and Dave might be jealous, and even this isn't without its savour of pleasure.

Mainly this meeting will act to normalise the relationship between you and her—bring it back to earth. Showing her to Terry and David will be the necessary spell to prove her reality; she will be seen and accepted at large. It's the next step which has been so far lagging. And it will also, simultaneously, be the incantation needed to break her too-powerful hold over you and to dispel the horror of your closeness; by letting your masculine, trusted friends into the frame so she no longer fills it entire you shall assert through them your independence, the boundaries of your own existence.

In a momentary flash, with an attendant shower of these bright justifications, all this becomes clear to you. After taking a few seconds of stupefied delight in the plan, you soar around the apartment in thoughtless, shallow glee, cleaning and arranging, carefully laying her out upright on the sofa, choosing the angle and the light that she should appear at her best.

You have always been a self-conscious host—a relic, probably, of years as a child being told to offer, under your mother's tutelage, bowls of nuts or crisps to adult guests, duties you first relished, then about which you felt ambivalent, and which you came finally to resent as a surly late-teen. When Terry and Dave finally arrive you have been twiddling your thumbs next to the doll on the sofa for months, years of enervated boredom, yet suddenly, as you hear the knock—too quick!, too quick! There are things one always has yet to do but which can only be thought of, it would seem, at the moment of the arrival of long-awaited guests. You run into the bathroom to spray on some aftershave, even though it will now be too obviously fresh, despite your technique of spraying it on your chest rather than your neck and trying to mute it underneath your shirt.

Terry and Dave arrive with beers and you usher them into the sitting room, leading the way and leaving Dave to shut the door behind him in a way that feels unmannerly and odd as soon as you've done it but which, you tell yourself, is probably imperceptible to the other two. Your heart at this point, until they notice her—which is taking a remarkably, almost impossibly long time, many seconds, even when they are now arrived in the sitting room—is going like the fucking clappers. They notice, and when they do you are glad of the beers they've brought, since that gives you something to do, and you take the bag from Dave, mid-conversation, and unpack it in the kitchen. You think you are being normal enough. You remove three beers and then arrange the rest in an extremely assiduous row in the fridge, partly out of a sense of hostly propriety, partly because you want to appear to be occupied whilst surreptitiously checking that they, particularly Terry, are looking at her.

Their surprise is delicious, though it briefly scares you to see Terry so shocked, left for once with nothing to say. It is both reassuring and tragic when he rapidly recovers mastery of the situation and starts to laugh uncontrollably. Was this whole thing a joke you were playing? You suppose it could have been. The idea of Terry is usually much nicer than Terry himself, and when you're apart you always seem to forget the realities of his scrawny, abrasive presence, rubbing the corners off everything.

Minutes go by in heady freefall, and you are made stunned by what you have done. An unanticipated thrill runs through you when they say how hot she is, and at first they are there simply staring at her agog and unabashed. But, after a period of understandably curious formal inspection, when she is no longer the topic of discussion she can't be so shamefacedly ogled. It is then that Terry performs, when he thinks you aren't watching, that visual slither particular to men, the glance which licks down the pale body from the face to the toes and back up again, swelling around whatever curves are found in between. Your gratification brings a tight smile irresistibly to your lips.

But after this, as everything sinks through you amid the chit chat, there's a sick feeling you try to suppress. For now, at least, you can keep it at bay, distracted by the flowing action of having friends in your home and having to host. You act as though everything is normal. Gigs. Girls. Gossip. Yet it is hard to sit still and you experience bodily relief, like the relief of vomiting, when the time comes to leave. On the way out you can see that Terry has been waiting to touch her, and he finds the excuse of a joke to grab her breasts very very hard, making a hooting noise.

"Bye Dolly!"

A fleck of spittle appears to travel from his soft, over-delicate lips and into her face. You have to laugh. On the way down the stairs you feel as though you are going to sick up your beer, and you must hide an erection.

Before the night out you've agreed upon—drinking to be done in Soho before probably catching a set at Ronnie's—Terry wants to pay a visit to a birthday party; it's just on the way; it won't take any time at all. The girl is called Liv, one of his old MA classmates. And it is, at least, nearby, at the De Hems Dutch pub, Macclesfield Street, on the outskirts of Chinatown. Liv has chosen to host it there, Terry says, because her boyfriend, Levi, is Dutch. Attached: Liv and Levi. They're practically anagrams.

Terry, regarding women, has always seemed aloof, and despite the fact that you've never seen him with any girlfriend you still have the impression he's rather good with women. Once or twice you've noticed him shiftily disappearing from a gig and thought you glimpsed a person leaving with him whose face you couldn't see. If asked the next morning whether he had frisked away with a girl there would always be a story, immediately divulged, and always featuring remarkable sex. You have previously made mental notes to ask him the same question when you've definitely seen him leave alone, but you never remember to do so.

In the top room of the pub, reserved for Liv's party, is a very 'Terry' sort of group. Most of them seem to have gone to the Courtauld together, and after presenting you to Liv, who is wearing a man's white shirt with braces and a blue bow tie, Terry fails to introduce you to any of the rest. It is, in one way, a relief, and luckily Dave is there for you to mill with undisturbed on the outskirts of groups as women wearing pashminas and librarian glasses and men in check shirts and big sweaters talk about supervisors, Shoreditch, cocktails, Michelangelo and sourdough. Amidst all this you keep worrying that Terry is going to spill the beans. You know Dave would never. You don't think he has, since except for the occasional glare from those in the party who can't place you in the group, meant to assert their place and yours, no one seems to be looking at you any more than usual—which is to say hardly at all. You can't work out how many of them know Terry, or indeed each other.

Thankfully you don't stay long, just for one drink as promised, but you can't slink off before the singing of *Happy Birthday*. Until the cake is brought out you haven't been able to spot Levi, but there he is now standing with Liv at the head of the table, barrel-like and hirsute. Undeserving, you decide, of the girlfriend uplit attractively by the candles of the tiny cake that three giggling girls have paraded across the room, and him smiling into the face of his smiling anagram. You and Dave are behind everyone else, a few metres apart from the group and the circle of candlelight, and as the singing starts up the scene begins to look as though it is happening somewhere else. As a detached observer you sense quite palpably the suspended moment during the singing of *Happy Birthday* when it has to be decided what to call Liv, or Livvy, or Olivia, in the song. First the loud confusion of conversations is suddenly interrupted by the rising chorus of the singing and this orchestrated, improvised moment comes crashing over the party like a possessing charm, a mounting tide hushing the clamour then channelling the hubbub together, and so the voicing of her name is something that it hasn't occurred to anyone, until the very second approaches, to preconsider, and they must suddenly calculate as a group what they are to call her, what everyone else is likely to call her, unless…

…there is this moment of total suspension when the candles seem to halt their flickering and rise upwards in suspenseful inhalation with the party—a terrible pause—before Levi barrels loudly over the rest, just in time, in a deep *basso profondo*: "Liiiivvyyy." Happy birthday, to you.

When the immediate furore has died down you gather behind Terry to watch him say his goodbyes to the host, and to wave yours unnoticed. He's rather too stylish about it, bordering on smarmy slickness as he leans in dramatically to administer a loud, puckered "mwah" of a kiss on each of Livvy's cheeks, making full use of his hands holding her shoulders, and you can't believe people aren't suspicious or even aware of how fulsome he is. Livvy is, of course, delighted. Terry leads the conversation on the way out down the single-file staircase; Dave answers him; you are silent.

As you pass Bar Italia on Frith Street a child runs away from the piped steel chairs and tables outside; he is three, perhaps, with loose brown curls, and his parents and a couple of what appear to be extended family members have stood up from their seats and are shrugging on coats and closing the clasps on bags. He has run a few steps ahead of them, knowing that since it is finally the time for departure he now has some licence to stray and can pretend that he is leading the way. He is out late—it is after nine—and as it is dusk on a Thursday at the end of Autumn the streets are red, luminescent bone and dusty in the dying light and are not yet overrun. It is the suspensory moment between the quiet, businesslike bustle of the day in slow-running sunshine and the faster but less purposeful movements of the night. This is the empty time and the changing of the guard, when the stage lights dim and show bright again with a new reddish tint as the night cast trip on. This toddler and his family look like Mediterraneans, Greeks maybe, and are bridging the gap onstage, some of the last to scamper off before the nighttide performers.

The toddler, who is wearing red dungarees, takes three or four juddering steps then trips and falls, with the sudden slap of hands and knees on pavement and the total pause that comes afterwards. His relatives have not seen. He gets to his feet. Looks down deeply at his palms. They are already red, and are peppered with pebbles and dirt. Still staring at his hands he walks back to the table, then he looks up and holds them out. His mother, at first, thinks he is showing her something he has found, but then she notices the palms and start to coo sympathy. Only now does his expression change. Until this point he was stunned and separate from his pain, his consciousness of self suspended, but he awakens to it now in seeing others' consciousness of him. You can't hear the conversation, but as she asks him what you imagine is whether he fell over he crams up his eyes, hands still held out in front of him, and begins to bawl. The whole scene takes but half a minute, then you pull your eyes away, your nose wrinkling at his disgusting tears.

In the drinks that follow the venues don't come singly but all together. Drink flows through the night, and in Soho that evening all the world seems to be getting drunk in tune. You have wondered, at parties or with friends, at the apparently self-regulating system of people getting drunk together; how rare it is for anyone to be markedly more drunk or sober than the rest. Amidst the mess of such an evening there exists a complex network of minute adjustments. Those three have a shot together; these onlookers decide to do the same. She feels too drunk for the conversation and has a glass of water. This one has just joined and looks sober, let's buy him a drink. Tonight this seems to be happening across the whole of Soho. Tonight these drunkards and you amongst them cross-pollinate promiscuously, spreading their inebriation as dust on the wind until all the groups in all the bars have been linked by chain touch. You feel bound together with these revellers, falling across Soho's square mile, in the small miracle of being in touching distance tonight.

One thing you have always wanted, a constant fantasy, is a barman who understands you. Who's so surly to all the other customers that it's an emotionally draining experience for them to get served, but who greets you with a nod and a grunt and puts your drink in front of you when you walk in. You want a hotel bar that's always open, where there are mahogany balustrades curving to support the countertop, a polished and dented sweep of wood immaculately cared for. Where glasses hang from brass rails above the bar. Where red lights from the street outside hang in the glasses, and as the cars go by their headlights make a squadron of lesser lights slide across those polished bulbs. And where no music plays. Café Boheme might be one of the bars in London nearest to this, but it is full, full, too popular. Especially tonight.

From this ideal scene of yours, however, it cannot be disputed that she has been taken entire.

It's probably the eighth or ninth drink. All three of you like drinking but none of you are drinkers, so by now you are all well on your way. Terry's gaze has come completely undone and he can hardly focus on you while you are talking, directing his eyes instead in your general direction or seemingly at odd parts of your face. Even Dave, enormous, has gone red in the face and his forehead has started to look glossy, the sparse hair taking on a dejected, even floppier, flaxier aspect than usual. You imagine that you look the most normal, but you are aware that your movements are slow and your eyes shiny, your speech a bit slurred. And it is in the very second of thinking this that you see her.

There is a woman at the bar who makes the world appear incidental to her existence, as if that lithe black dress washed against her skin as naturally and exactly as the line where sea meets sand. Things sparkle at her wrists and neck with light that darts up her bare arms, across her collarbone, and leaps her neck to run amok about her smile when she laughs open-mouthed, head back, showing jugular and throat. Around her eyes the smoky mascara looks perfectly careless, merely the natural incident of the grey blue stones that burn there, necessitating ash.

Her eyes catch yours by accident across the bar—of course she's not interested—and almost decimate you offhand. In a second you are made collateral to a world to which you thought you had a right. You desperately hope she has a boyfriend, that there is not the taunt of her availability there to spoil the world. You know, looking at her, that your greatest hope is for a woman with eyes that have any cinder of the presence of hers, for a woman whose eyes might, once or twice in a marriage, mean something with the significance with which hers burn constantly tonight.

You stagger to the loo. As the door with the porthole window at the top of the stairs swings closed behind you the sound is muffled one degree. Descending the stairs to the basement it quietens another; when the door of the gents closes it drops still further to a low shaking buzz. Although you only need to piss you enter the cubicle for privacy, and there is the sound of water gushing in pipes around you, underground, and the vague trampling of upstairs. If Terry died up there, you realise, or screamed at the top of his lungs, you wouldn't hear him. One is so quickly muffled and alone and it is all at once extraordinary, as you piss, how quickly people grow smaller and quieter and recede and finally disappear when you take your leave of them. Closing up the dolls' house door of their existence they become miniature, and then the house itself folds up as you walk away. It becomes suddenly astonishing to your reason that one can find anyone again at all, in the way we do it by finding a circle, then a circle in that circle, and a circle in that circle's circle. The world, Europe, Britain, London, Soho, the corner of Greek Street and Old Compton Street, number 17, at the bar on the right when you come in, leaning on the zinc, that glitter in her eye the way that muscle moves it at the corner. Then you just walk away, fold them together and telescope them all back into themselves.

You slip out, steering clear of the bar and keeping the crowd between you and your friends there. You're relying on the general drunkenness to obscure your disappearance, and on your sober self tomorrow to be able to formulate a convincing excuse for it that you can't think of now. As you push open the thick main door, head down to hide your face from the bar, the tall black bouncer in the trilby bids you goodnight—just as he would any other client leaving. And yet…there are so many other people tearing in and out and he doesn't seem to be saying it to them; you wonder if he is being ironic because he knows you're trying to slink away. But you've already shouldered out to make a hard right and are walking with the forward-leaning march of drunkenness towards Shaftesbury Avenue, that walk in which one's knees seem especially stiff and satisfying to stamp open in front to catch you at each step. Your hands are in the pockets of your overcoat and tugged down to your groin to keep the lapels tight to your neck in the chill wind. It's not good for saxophonists to catch colds. You doze in the taxi. Pausing halfway up the stairs to your door with the effort of composition, swaying a little, you write Terry and Dave a message on your phone to the effect that you threw up in the loo and got sick and went home and sorry. With what you think of, in your current state, as great canniness you calculate that they're significantly more likely to believe a tale involving some disgrace to yourself.

She's there where you left her, but you aren't ready to begin the scene yet; you go to the kitchen and down a glass of water, drink a second in a few gulps, then let the tap run until it flows very cold—too cold to down—and take sips from a third, placing it on the counter between the sips and staring at it, pressing your palms to the cool Formica.

When you do go to her you kneel in front of the sofa to press her hand and kiss her cool cheek, in apology for the evening or for something about to come. You murmur into her neck some nothings you no longer remember or which you have chosen to forget.

When you started making love to her, how you began, or brought her to the bedroom, or took your clothes off, or got the candle lit on the bedside table as you stared into her eyes, you don't know. But you come to, and find yourself poised above her. There is an island of consciousness from that night which stays with you, which you can look at in memory still—one of those moments. The way she moved under you that night, the way you and she moved together, the way all moved as you lay still. As you move with her the bedcovers start to rustle like the sand pulled back and forth by the sea: the old to and fro where all ends and begins. For one long, moronic moment your reality blurs a little, and her face looks both focussed and sidereal, and there is a moment when you are sure that she's going to speak. Not to speak in your imagination as she has been doing, but literally to speak, and you stare into her face, haloed by your adrenaline puncturing the drunkenness and giving her an otherworldly ascendant quality as though rising out of a dark lake, the candlelight animating her features and making them appear to move with the light against the black, arterial red of the sheets in the dim dull darkness. As she shimmers there, face moving as under a heat haze, your fear rises, a fear of her speaking, and a knot of other, complex emotion all rises, and your nightmarish terror is only kept in check by occasionally calling yourself back to wakefulness, to channel your drifting thoughts, like trying to drive when drunk. And then, quite suddenly, or taking a very long time, your thoughts snap from their moorings and drift out—by the time you have any awareness of it at all, have already drifted.

You have no idea of the interim—if it is seconds or many minutes—while you're still fucking her, between this moment of terror that she will speak and finding yourself lost a little—lost a lot. She has been staring into you, you have been staring into her, moving with her, all moving, and you have been swimming out to sea on one of your beach holidays in Greece when you were a child. Swimming out to sea, in sight of your parents but alone, conjured by them not to swim out too far, you turn back to face the shore and it is there, metres away, you could put your feet down as soon as you liked, really. So you swim out further, a little while, thinking of nothing. Time passes. You swim. You float. Until a sudden cold halts you. You look down, and the water below you has darkened to black blue, your feet barely visible over the void, kicking weakly in it, barely keeping above it, and anything could be below you and anything could come out from there. And then you look up and there is just horizon, horizon, horizon, and as the waves come one by one you can barely see what's behind them, and you don't know how far out you are for perspective has ceased to exist at all. Your ears try to ground you, but even stretching your neck out from the waves you cannot hear any of the voices or hubbub of the shore. You turn, panicked, back towards it and see everything on the beach made miniature, for no good reason, for you only have to look the other way and geometry ends. In this stirring place fears and flurries wash over you—in sight, nevertheless, of normality, but cut off from it as if from a world through a mirror—only dumb sight penetrates—and you could shout and scream and be the only one to hear it. When you put your head down and thrash at the shore, limbs light with adrenaline, sometimes your knees scrape pebbles at once and you are immediately there, being toppled from standing by the waves. At others it seems so close and you paddle and paddle and look up with the salt in your eyes and many minutes have gone by and you have made no progress at all—before you suddenly gain it without warning. In this half space, with her in the bed, your fears and hopes proliferate. Love. Falling for this doll. Seeing yourself waste away. Whether your limbs will cramp. Not finding your lover. A sudden riptide tearing you out to sea. Finding your lover. But all is safe and warm as the sea rages.

And, finding yourself warm amidst her and hanging over her you push her legs back, and as you do so something snags, then snaps. A hawser at her hip. As it goes, cracking from the tension, you beach yourself between her thighs, and there is a salty pain at the end of your penis which seems of a kind with the wince squeezing your tear ducts. The latter are crying: thick, childish tears pushed forward by a sour pressure behind your eyes. You heave and roll with a big shuddering sob, and there is a deep sweet hurt you can't do anything about.

You autopilot to the bathroom to clean yourself off. You'll clean her tomorrow. When you come back you notice a rip in the silicone at the front of the doll's pelvis. You're too tired and disconnected to care. Sleep happens somehow, somewhere, as if to someone else; not the sleep that heals but a desolate, ambiguous oblivion, both shallow and deadly still.

You wake to a feeling of disgust before you have even opened your eyes. You are awash with it; it has seeped into your corners and soaked you through during the night. Your sleep has rested you not at all, and you feel you are merely on the very surface of things, the scum of things, a person only in the most perfunctory way. Hangover is a good term for this ghostly suspension. This is how easy death would be, you think—it's just a fading of the picture, like this but further, a little further, until you're gone altogether.

Lying in the bed you remember the night. The doll is next to you and clumsy in the covers, you're sure of it. You can sense her there but you can't bear to look. What were you thinking, bringing them here to see her; bringing her out to see them? And yet—although in your state of still-drunkenness you don't yet trust your ability to imagine the responses of others with any realism—you can't picture anything but normalcy for your next meeting with your friends. Empathy is effortful and this morning it has left. In its wake—disgust.

Quickly you locate your disgust on the doll. Her nudity last night was appalling, pressing outwards from the surroundings onto your attention. The image of her sitting so primly upright and lurid on the sofa as Terry and Dave poked and prodded her is horrific now, a nightmare, and she feels tarnished by their touch. How could she have let them do that to her? Had she liked it? She can only have liked it, or enjoyed some part of it, if she was there being so passive and taking it. And for you to have thought to bring her out in the first place she must have wanted it, or a part of her a part of it. You hate these jealous fixations. You know they're irrational. You feel that even by thinking them you might bring them into being and make them true and yet you can't stop, you fret the thoughts remorselessly. Did she prefer them to you? The way Terry spoke in her face, took hold of her nipple, was so possessive. Did she think he was handsome? Enjoy his gaze? Their eyes have been all over her. Now that she has seen those others—perhaps she won't want you. Terry mainly, of course, but Dave's lumbering size is maybe attractive, the need to be thumped around by someone, something massive.

You are decided. Out of the static comes resolution. You do not think—in fact you suppress thought—you merely act. Shower. Clothes. Even moisturising cream under eyes, sliming the dark half-moons. On the street you ignore your hungover paranoia and listen, for once, to the sensible part of you saying that no one is thinking anything of you, that you don't look any different from usual. No one thinks much of a man buying two coffees—the second to imply some explanation to any onlookers of what you are to purchase next: a bunch of make up at Superdrug. You don't scrutinise yourself; it ain't allowed. Possibly there's a need to claim her. Perhaps there's a need to paint over last night. But no need to concern yourself with that. In your half-drunken state you are still permitted to lose yourself a little.

When you first apply the make up it is slow. It is deliberate. You don't plan to put it all on, necessarily; you just want to doll her up a bit in order, you tell yourself, to make up for last night. You apply the foundation and her face changes colour; the others didn't see her like this. This is for you. But you grow pale with sudden doubt—is it? The foundation doesn't match the skin tone of her neck; try to bleed it in. Still doesn't look good. She's not doing it for you herself. Your ears feel hot at the lobes. You are having to do it to her. Forget about that. You take up the blusher and its brush. You just wish she desired you enough to do this. Tease her for it. "Now for your blusher, my dear" you say. The words catch in your throat as you have not spoken for a while; their false cheerfulness echoes brashly in the room, then crashes into the silence. You take up the clean brush and frisk it at her face, dabbing it at her, rustling it into her eyes, pretending to play but taking out some kind of frustration under the guise of frivolity, enjoying pressing the irritating filaments amongst her eyelashes. You dip it in the blusher with an excess of vigour and some of it puffs up onto your cuff. You try to blow it off, but a factory rose tint smear remains. You feel the blood rising to your face in annoyance.

You whisk on the blusher with rapid flicks of the wrist. You try to be offhand, but exceed your artisanship; too much has gone on and it hasn't blended in. Is this good light in which to be working? You look up at the lightbulb too suddenly and it stings your eyes. Too late anyway. You blend it in as well as you can by blowing and with smart touches. Possibly it can be fixed with the eyeliner. Perhaps that's the order you're supposed to do these things in anyway; eyeliner first, bring the complexion up to meet the eyes. Have you read that somewhere or merely imagined it? You take up the eyeliner pencil and try it on your finger. It works better than you had imagined; your finger's marked. Damn. Briskly you drag the pencil across her skin, with an efficiency of movement which sacrifices her comfort to speed. So what if the delicate skin under her eyes is tugged and roughed a bit? She looks a little better. You kiss her. Deeply. That *is* better. Bitch.

Leaning over to pick up the mascara you catch sight of yourself in the hand mirror. You have a black mark on your cheek where you must have touched your face with the eyeliner finger. Fuck. Oh well. How are you going to take any of this off, come to think of it? You prepare to apply her mascara, hand trembling now. It's hard to get the right amount of black goop on the bristles so it's not overladen, and wiping it on the rim of the thin tube it comes in distributes the mascara unevenly across the brush. You don't even know how to do this. You chump. Your shaking hands smear mascara on the bottom of her iris where it meets the white. You want to fuck her for making you desire her so painfully. You try to rub it off with an indelicate, moistened thumb and end up smearing it across the glassy white of her eye, clumsily gumming some of the eyelashes together below. You hear a woman's laugh in the street, and then another. You're having to do all this because nobody will put make up on for you. This is a mask that passion would crack; the bloom on the butterfly that wingbeats would shrug off. For the only true state of a made up face is in perfect repose. Artifice prevents action; any real feeling and this face would begin to fall off. You grab her chin, hard, with one hand and shake it quickly from side to side, feeling a pressure behind your eyes and the colour rising to your cheeks.

Fuck; fuck. You wipe your thumb on your jeans without thinking first, or maybe just reckless of the result, and the mascara no doubt stains them. You start to hate her as you do this make up all wrong, full of your hopeless, male indelicacy. You oaf. And then you hate yourself for hating her. She seems to be mocking you, allowing you to paint her. Still keeping whatever it is that you're trying to take away. Where is she hiding it? You take up the lipstick with intent, nearly wild now, a cough in your throat that is like a laughing sob, and you press the stick hard on her lips, blunting the wax against her and watching the end flake as you, eyes stinging, push out your own lips in a mocking, kissing pout, with suddenly trembling face, eyes and cheeks wincing up into bitterest sob, still continuing to try to mock as really your own face breaks down and falls out of your control. You want to take her by the throat and squeeze as though you might suffocate there your own rising sobs, your own difficulty breathing. With her neck in your hand you lean in, mouth distraught and ragged with sudden, unexpected grief and frustration at a thing you cannot place but which finds itself in her, or the space between your mouths, and you press your lips hard against hers—a kiss done for companionship and not artistry, at first, a tear squeezed from between your too-tight eyes dripping, you can feel, into the sand and red of her complexion. But then, in an access of grief where you abandon yourself to satire, a weeping joke that does not laugh but ennobles itself by joking without laughter to point at truth, you move your head from side to side—kissing her 50s movie heroine style—and come away. The hand mirror. You look, as they never do in films, as though you have been punched in the mouth and your lips have bled out with the shock like bruised fruit—and so does she. Guffaw loud, then, at both of you, a laugh in bitter sadness and hatred. You still want her—there is nothing you can do to gain her—you can paint on her but not so force her to your conceit as to make her to want—or to stop you from wanting her.

And then, quite suddenly, her chin is in your left hand, and your right is drawing back, ever so slowly, to belt the doll across the face. Your hand is moving back, drawing back to prepare for the strike, in the manner with which people mime their tennis strokes or pretend to hit each other in slow motion. There has been a moment of blind fury, and you have found yourself possessed of this blow. But as soon as the idea hits you—you are, just as suddenly, tired. Countenancing the violence is enough. Your hand slows slower still. Facing the desire to strike is its own respite. And as quickly as it came it is exhausted. The deepest fatigue; total expiation; your limbs are heavy as a drowned man logged with water or as limbs of wood. You complete the action and bring your hand to caress her face—it were a strike but for its slowest speed—and clap your fingers, gently, twice, against her cheek, chucking her, your eyes glazing into a distance where nothing is found but thought.

Gradually, her lips smeared to the side, you notice that she begins to change. Under your eyes she starts a metamorphosis, abstracted from herself and her usual look by the make up, and it's not wonderful but awful. Under the edge of your gaze, like peering into a funhouse mirror, she begins to morph into your image of desire thrown back.

With the approach of the vision but before it arrives comes a dread that starts in your stomach, and then begins to plummet when you find the insight confirmed. You look at her. Confirmed again. You take a staggered step backward. There too. Your eyes are moving rapidly now, all over her body from point to point, and your mouth has come to hang open in an expression of slack shock.

She is...

she is just...

As when a cloud passes in front of the sun and the afternoon tea becomes grim and unbearable, the coffee turning cold in the cups and the sky drab and lifeless, thus she changes before you. Your desire has risen to its height and crashed, and all at once you can see the wires of this show, all clear to you as never before. Wearing the make up she comes away from herself, and you see her for what she is—just a doll.

Your eyes find her lips. One pair, indifferent pink, but coloured and phrased by all the lips you knew before you ordered these, the colours of those other lips bleeding through. Lips pleated to kiss yours or sneering with pleasure. Lips glossed in magazine photographs, others by licking. You've been turned on by these doll's lips because they find lips you've known. Their pastel colour, the way they can form a seal around your cock and be pulled out by it in vacuum suction: there is a moment of Elena, and whatever other girls had her style of sucking, that particular effect enabled by the absence of fat on the face which, in Elena, was a general index of her athletic, runner's form. But Elena's lips were relatively thin over big teeth, and she smiled with the deepest dimples; in this doll the dimples are almost there, the teeth and thinness not. For rather than taut over teeth this doll's lips hang, when not in use, in a phrase of mouth that looks paused to make a face that's questioning: and there is Marie, her lips pushed forward in French phonemes to come away from the teeth a touch or pouted, or perhaps it is the woman you saw last week in a café who shared that language and the phrase of mouth.

Ankles: cockable. Wrists: ibid. There is a Cockney fruit seller in the market near your apartment. On weekends she stands under the tarpaulin, dusky and tan in her apron beneath the dripping rain. She is the most attractive obese woman you have ever seen, her breasts enormous, her bottom at large; but her face is not fat and nor are her wrists. The latter, you realise now, enthral you. You have, you also discover, ordered fruit just to watch them. They are delicately-boned like a pencil sketch done too thin. Dropping oranges with careless backhand into crisp paper bags; the way her hands fall in languorous extension and slight ulnar deviation. Here they are in the doll.

The doll's hair isn't hers either. It is the hair of women you've known, or not even known but wanted, or not even fully wanted but whose hair…in the way the doll's hair falls in curtains it is the hair of women you've been crammed against in tube carriages, your nose nearly in the bouquets of their necks. Hair from wet days in the Underground amidst the stink of coats; not women you want, necessarily—women whose faces you never see—but women whose hair, despite yourself, puts hands on your lust when you smell its shampoo mingled with the sweet scent of scalp.

Tits: not what you've known but what you were never able to possess. The way they meet the doll's chest at their underside, coming away from the ribcage horizontally then up without any sag or downward fall; it's a boob job effect you've never seen in reality but only on pornstars in movies or hinted at beneath the shirts of strangers. Her slightly puffy nipples have something of a woman you saw once at the beach in Greece; she was tanned, frolicking thigh-deep in the waves with someone, maybe her boyfriend, you don't remember. You must have been thirteen and she was probably nineteen or twenty, now you come to think on it; barely older than you were, it seems in retrospect, but at the time much older in every way that mattered. She was topless, splashing water over her big, tanned breasts and making sure (you're now certain of it) to shake them around. Her areolae, in particular, had a soft, inflated-deflated look to them. You chose your doll's nipples because, you know it now, they had something of this picture of lust. Cerulean Pink SUPER PUFFY L.

Her silhouette shifts, in and out of form. You find in it, flickering, the silhouettes of thousands of women you've known, or not known but wanted, sketched over and over again on top of each other and rubbed out and sketched again in air and then compiling, overlapping, averaging out, overlaid and dream-softened into the sfumato totality of what you most want, whether you know it or not. These old desires that you spot in her lips, limbs, tits, are only those you recognise explicitly, but most of it goes much deeper than that. Behind them, shadow-stacked behind her, are all the shades of the forgotten, the millions of women who've turned you on or—with the pressure of space upon sculpture—who've done the opposite, but shifted now into plastic. She's an armature for memory, and whilst specific, identifiable shreds of it hang on her in scrim, the main flesh of the figure is agglomerated with the liquid plaster of unconscious desire; forms diving down in the memory, through specificity, to vagueness, to shadows, to the absolute dark.

Last, you look at her eyes. Their vulnerable blue; their transparency. These, you realise now, you chose because Marge had big, doe-dark eyes, and this doll's are the opposite. The mascara you've smeared on emulates the smoky, dirty, barfly look of that woman last night. But none of these things really belong to the doll; no wrinkles made, no attitudes formed of her own expression. Part of what's arousing about her is all this resonance, but not now, when you see the strings; you liked her only for the ways in which she is not herself. This isn't love but its opposite.

And so, in this moment which is years of memory compounded out of time, she is a piece of plastic again. Shock and disbelief at your own need for this lump of hard rubber and steel happen somewhere, but you aren't ready to feel them yet. Head hung, you reach without seeing for the hand mirror and hold it up to her face—and then you give her a shove. The doll falls backwards with the chair beneath it. And before you know it, as you watch it tip, you are in the dark of the doll. You fall into its chest somewhere and a part of you falls with it, in complete darkness, unable to move but moving, falling back with the chair already.

There are two places like this movement in the dark. Lifts and the carriages of the Underground have this in common: they are the two places we regularly find ourselves where one has the sensation of movement without sight of movement or bearings; without the ability to apprehend place. And they are also between places; places whose only purpose for existence is to take you somewhere else. Falling in the dark of the doll your eyes close to yourself and you are on the London Underground.

For you the carriages of the Underground are not places of purgatory but places of dream; places that cease to be real places as the platform slips by into flat, deep darkness that presses its face and slides its brow against the windows of the carriage; places where, because you cannot go any faster or control your course any longer, you are relieved of the responsibility of human worries. Here, in this rising car, you can do nothing to make it go faster or slower; your fate is no longer in your own hands and there's an intermission in your will, a lacuna in your otherwise self-possessed life. Here, in this train carriage, your purposes and the other places in which you exist are abstract, non-topographical, relating to a world reduced merely to dots or checks and strange names on a map of coloured lines, routes branching theoretically underground. The outside, upstairs world is a thing apart. Here that world is the dream, here where outside places relate to each other only through the thinnest lines drawn between them. The evidence of their existence is unconvincing; it is the difference between musical notation and rich, fat notes actually falling on the ear…or perhaps the other way around. The difference between G4 on a stave and Trane's sustained, wavering, delicately reiterated opening note on *Ev'ry Time We Say Goodbye* is as the rift between the firm existence of this metal carriage with its strangers and that other world above of which the station names speak: insurmountable.

And it is down here that you have been searching. You walk all the way along the platform, in case she's waiting at the other end, obscured by the crowd. For if you don't find her there you may otherwise be locked together into adjacency in the carriages you mount, one following the other but kept in rigid distance; unable to see each other because you're being held so close. You see a woman with her silhouette walking ahead of you towards the end of the platform, or descending the stairs in front, and you quicken your pace to overtake her so you can look at her face. But the woman turns and is not her, and sometimes this is more surprising than if it were; as when, when you were a child, you approached a woman in the supermarket you thought was your mother, only to be brought up sharp starkly to meet a reality that had no regard for your conception of it when that person turned and, monstrously, was not her but—another.

And then, because she is not there amongst the persons on the platform, you must embark alone. You take your seat and the platform begins to move past, passing out of space, and, as it passes, your eyes flit nystagmic with the crowd passing on the platform the train is passing as it passes the platform, a part of you asleep and dreaming of seeing her. And as your carriage enters the tunnel and the dark approaches, taking irrevocably fleet steps down the train towards you as the windows entering the tunnel darken and go out one by one down the carriages, you see her, just turning away, just missing the train, and you start to your feet wide-eyed and grasping for the handrail, just as all is wiped into black. Flat black. Matt black. A thrum into darkness. The graffiti cut into the windows leaps out at you as it is lit against the black outside, and again you are sent hurtling through the dark.

For a moment, now, when you are in the dark of the doll on the Underground, you see what is really the case, always. One is simply falling through darkness without will or direction, falling in her chest with the chair—as she plummets back her hair falls slower, splayed like water's upsplash, buoyed on the air, but then pulled down with her—falling through lift shafts without bearing, falling queasily off the earth's slant as it spins you around and around, the earth falling through space like a stone playing in a well, a random spattering of shattered crystal; a glass dropped by a god in the night.

* * *

After this, you leave the doll lying there on the floor. You enter one of those reasonless periods of no clarity, no time, no memories. You can't muster the strength to face up to what you have done by making a decision, to make yourself pick her up or tidy anything else, but your suspended state is restful this time, not frantic. Once again best-before dates suddenly cycle into the past, and dust piles up on surfaces you thought you had cleaned just yesterday. But it's the blanketing of rest, not the rot of decay, and you don't experience the fallen dust or the doll, the plates and dishes, the laundry pooling on the floor, as a weight crushing you that you must strain against, but as a blanket pressing you down and which you do not resist, interring you under dust, burying you at the bottom of a sea bed in a way that is ultimately restful, not anxious, in its thoughtlessness. When you decline you want to decline like this: do, done, dust. The sediment that builds up around and over you in your flat in these minutes, days, weeks, who knows, only appears to push you more into yourself, to make you part of its strata. It isn't dirty or rotting in its compression of you and of the apartment, but clean; a clean dust falling over everything. The clocks run out of time, the hands go limp and splay themselves randomly across the faces, out of relation to you, and even the clouds behind the curtains slump into each other and make a mess of the sky. You don't resist. You feel warm and comfortable here. Here there is the solace and the silence of the seabed; the solace of giving up.

But, before long, you begin to be stirred by the slower tides at the bottom of this ocean, the sand dust shifting over your form pressed face-down into the ocean floor. You don't snap out of it suddenly and unstably, as you have done from such moods before—awaking into consciousness as a sleeping person dropped in freezing water. This time you repair gradually, coming back to yourself one thought at a time. First you are able to move more freely, the sand falling away. Then you are able to shower, to clean off the last vestiges of silt. Then, soon, to shave. To dress. Before long you wash a coffee cup before you make the coffee in it. Before much longer, you can desire a coffee, rather than desiring just the desire for one. Soon you aren't merely going through the motions but starting to mean them, just a little.

During this period the doll remains on the floor, and whilst at the commencement you cannot allow yourself to think about her, after a while has passed—who knows how long—the sand and dust have begun to bury her a bit. She has become less of a person, a presence, lying there beneath that dust, form splayed on the floor on top of the upset chair, hair and arms spread as though still falling—this is no longer the diorama of a tragic drama but merely a collection of objects, without the possibility for significance or guilt; a set of thoughts and private fantasies you once indulged— and who would hold themselves responsible for what they once dreamt?

As soon as you are able to look at her at all you are careful, at first, to try to look at her only wistfully—and then you don't need to try but simply do. She's a childhood toy, still holding some place in your affection, but wilfully you press those emotions down and turn away from the sting of pain which all of us feel about our pasts, the shame of having once been so small, and of the things that we now discard having once meant so much.

One day you wake up with the desire to buy groceries. To find healthy food in your fridge in crisp packets of cellophane, to throw out the yellowed hemisphere of mozzarella in its cut plastic sac that is stuck to the inside of the top shelf and the bulb of garlic next to it, wizened in on itself in an arthritic fist, and instead to find bright, organised shapes and vegetable vitality when you open the door. You also go grocery shopping because you know that, once bought, the groceries will themselves exercise some pressure to clean out the fridge; the pressure you need to unleash the cascade—and before long you are back, a full bag of groceries on the counter, wanting to clean your apartment. You have got a take-away cappuccino in a cardboard cup: large, even a shake of cocoa. You feel capable. And you are ready to shift the load pressing down upon all of the apartment; the load preventing the dishes from rising from the surfaces where they are stacked in architecture compiled over days; the weight entrancing the dirty clothes so they stick, static, to the floor; the slothfulness pulling back the corner of the sweet-smelling bedsheet that is coming away indecently to show the corner of the mattress. You are ready to shift her heavy body from on top of all of this and start.

You pick her up, your hands under her armpits. You make yourself treat her as though she were any other object, as though she weren't a human at all or even a human form. You look at her not in her eyes but with the callousness of the puppeteer who has ceased to believe his own act long ago, the only one for whom the spell is broken, so long has he been watching the secret workings of the wires that fall from his hands to the limbs of the puppets. It is thus that you try to watch and hold her, taking especially slow care in looking at her feet as you pull her up that they don't thwack the bedpost; moving her as though she were a very expensive and delicate object but with a disinterested care that is as polite, as flatly pragmatic as it is insulting—or would be to any human held so clinically by one they had loved, or been loved by, or…but you don't think of that now.

It is with this care for something secret, something of expense, that you fold it into the closet; as if putting beautiful old jewels away in a bank. The vacant top shelf of the walk-in cupboard has a small apse in the left corner at the very top, the contents of which are invisible from below. It is there that you shelve the doll. You have to fold it, to pick up the heels in your left hand and the back of its neck in your right, press the feet towards the face, and climb a small stepladder with it bundled like this, to fit it in between the shelf and the ceiling. You are pleased to leave it in a position that doesn't look human, even though it will damage and crease her joints and flesh—the renunciation seems all the fuller that way. Its legs are almost behind its head. Then you climb off the stepladder, pull the cord to turn off the light, and close the door.

A week or two later it is winter. And, when you can bear it and because you have to, you're on the Underground again. It's different now; pulled by the ghost of habit you still find your gaze snagged by the sleek outline of an imagined lookalike on the platform, but you blink and look down at your feet, or check the time until your train, and smile forgetfully to yourself. You have your saxophone in its case.

And then, in the twinkle of a Santa Claus' smile, you are in the courtyard of Somerset House, playing sax in a band next to the ice rink where the skaters are skating. There is a slight reverb in the courtyard, a slight reechoing as the music loops back off the walls, which the drums hit with a clatter and the piano with a tinkle of glass and the sax with a gasp. Until, that is, it begins to snow. The way snow comes down is not like rain. Rain can come so fast that it is not raining one moment and raining the next. Even with a first few drops, drops that you imagine like streaks or snips in the air, it is already beginning to rain. When it snows there is no clear beginning or end—sometimes one errant snowflake will drift away past you on the balustrade and into the cold air, and that will be it: no snow will come. At others there will be one, and then another, dancing together until they are joined by the troupe of which they are the vanguard, the first few revellers announcing the arrival of the silent procession of them all, melding with each other and dancing apart as they fall. Now it starts to snow so gradually, and then the effect of the snow is so slow. Snow white, slow white, there is no single point at which the world turns, turns white, but it is as though god is turning up the brightness, over-exposing the photograph ever so slowly, snowy, until it is already there and already has been there and you can't say precisely when the world wasn't white all along. As it snowed and you played jazz it fell into your saxophone, and into the hair and woollen hats of the skaters, and onto the eyelashes of young teenage girls who weren't pretending to be anything but children because they were with their mothers and it was Christmas, and it fell on the tiles of the roofs, and on the cobbles of the courtyard, and on the stone balustrades around, and on the ice and the gazebos, white on white. As it fell the reverb disappeared, turned down so gradually, slowly, snowy, as the snowy cobbles and roofs and the snow in the air took up the sound, swathed it round with a blanket, tucked it away and out of sight, and for a second you were playing jazz in infinity, in a stretch of very infinite space, all auditory perspective vanished into thick air, and if you closed your eyes you were in a place that was both close and warm and also immensely distant; you were at your grandfather's house again, in his drawing room, sitting on his knee and looking at him through your long dark curls and listening to him talk about the Speaking Clock, and he sat there with the errant threads of his kippah curling wildly away from his forehead, and the snow falling on him, and getting caught in his long dragon's eyebrows and in the curling white hairs on his cheeks, and making a little round cap on his kippah and shaking off in all directions when he laughed. And you are watching him through your curls and feeling your fingers on the saxophone lily-pad keys, and listening to the music and to his laugh, and you don't need to think to listen the music is simply a part of you, your whole being, playing is effortless, you're immensely sad with a sadness you wouldn't want to lose, and you can hear the infinite space of the courtyard and your grandfather's tattered drawing room, and you are there once again as the snow alights on the lashes of closed eyes. And you forget yourself and.

Disappear.

For exclusive discounts on Matador titles,
sign up to our occasional newsletter at
troubador.co.uk/bookshop